Slow Burn

A Sin City Novel

Isabel Morin

Chapter One

"CPA, huh? You don't think slogging around with a band will be too low-brow for you?"

Beth sat up straighter and looked Stu Mirsky in the eye. "This is exactly the sort of thing I've been looking for." This wasn't strictly true, since the idea of touring with a band had never occurred to her. But the spirit of it was true. As soon as she'd seen the post from another Ohio State alum on Facebook, she'd wanted the job.

"Plus," she went on, "I have skills you can use. You won't find anyone as detail-oriented or organized as me. If you wanted I could keep track of expenses and make sure you stay on budget. I can do everything you need, and I'll get to see some of the country while doing it. It's a perfect fit."

Stu signaled the waitress for more coffee and sat back against the vinyl seat. A big man in his mid-to late-thirties with curly brown hair, he seemed weary, as if this were the first rest he'd had in days. The interview was taking place in a diner, but Beth was too on edge to eat anything. She hadn't even known about this job until three days ago, but now that she was here, it seemed like the only thing worth doing.

"I'm not so sure about that," Stu said, rubbing at the dark circles under his eyes. "But I can't afford to be picky. I also can't afford to hire someone and have her run off in the middle of the tour."

"You run that risk with anyone, but I can tell you I'm the last person who would do that. Besides, I can take anything for four weeks."

He sat back in his seat and gave her an appraising look. "You'll be doing a lot of lifting. Helping with equipment and gear, that sort of thing. Not to mention driving long hours with guys who might not be your cup of tea and running errands that are way beneath you."

"That won't be a problem. The whole point is to try something different. And as you can see, I'm not exactly frail."

He didn't dispute this. She was five foot ten with broad shoulders and decent muscle tone. No one considered her dainty.

"Bringing a pretty woman into a band is probably the dumbest thing I could do," he said, as if reminding himself. He took a sip of coffee and winced, then drank some more. He looked her in the eye. "The guys are going to hit on you, I guarantee it. You may even want to take one of them up on it. I need you to promise me you won't."

"The thought of hooking up with a guy right now literally turns my stomach. I'm at the beginning of a very long break from men."

"I'll have to take your word for it," he said, looking doubtful. "What kind of car do you drive?"

"Uh, I drive a Subaru Outback," she said, embarrassed to admit she had a station wagon. But a co-worker had been selling it for a great deal.

His eyes narrowed. "How many miles on it?"

"Fifty-six thousand."

"Fine, you're hired."

***

Beth burst through Cheryl's door. " I got a job," she squealed.

Cheryl was sitting on the couch grading papers. Or she had been. Beth's abrupt entrance had surprised her, and now the papers were scattered across the floor and under the coffee table. Beth got down on her knees and helped pick them up.

"That's amazing," Cheryl said, giving her a hug. She stacked the papers and sat back down. "What will you be doing? Is it another accounting firm?"

Beth took a seat, then popped right back up again, too excited to sit still. "Well, no. I decided I needed a little adventure first. It's just a month-long thing, though, so even if it's crazy, it won't be forever."

"What is this mystery job?"

"A while back I friended a bunch of random alums on the Ohio State Facebook page. This one guy, Will Rogowski, is in a band, and a few days ago he posted that one of the guys touring with them had broken his ankle and they needed someone with a car who could travel with the band and help out. I wouldn't have thought anything of it, except that they were playing Las Vegas tonight. I emailed Will and he helped set up my interview today with the band's manager."

"Wait a second. Are you saying you're going *on the road?*"

"Yes. I'll finally see some of the country, and I'll get paid to do it." She paused. "Well, not paid exactly, but they'll take care of my room and board and reimburse me for gas."

"What will you be doing exactly?" Cheryl asked, looking doubtful.

"I'll be helping sell stuff at shows, sending out press kits, making sure they have food. That sort of thing, plus a lot of driving. It's not exactly rocket science. The guy who was doing it was an alcoholic high school drop-out."

"When do you leave?"

"Um, tomorrow morning."

"Seriously?" Cheryl sat up straight, her pretty face falling.

"I know. I'm sorry it's so sudden."

She could see Cheryl was trying to be excited for her, but it was costing her. They'd been friends since elementary school and were more like sisters. Cheryl had even lived with Beth's family through high school after her own family fell apart. Both of them had been thrilled by the prospect of living in the same city again, and now Beth was taking off.

She sat down next to Cheryl, exhausted by the ups and down of the day. "It's only for a little while. I'll be back before you know it."

"I'm sorry. I don't mean to be a downer. It's just that you've only been here a week."

"I know. But I think I need this. I feel like if I don't do something drastic, I'll end up with the exact kind of life I left behind." She looked down at her capable hands, the nails short and unpainted. "I'm just so tired of being careful all the time."

Cheryl blew out a long breath and moved closer, wrapping and arm around Beth's shoulders and hugging her close. "Funny, I always envied you all that stability, but I guess it has its downsides."

"Yeah. Maybe I should have followed you here and gotten a job stripping, too."

"Oh my God, your parents would have had heart attacks. I would have had a heart attack."

"You don't think I can be wild?" Beth asked, trying not to look disappointed.

"Being wild isn't all it's cracked up to be. Besides, I always liked having you as an example of the life I wanted to have. Something good and real, something to be proud of."

Beth blinked away tears. "Well, now you're the shining example for me. You certainly have better taste in men."

Cheryl smiled, but it was an inward smile, and Beth could tell she was thinking of Jason. "Just better luck."

"Maybe some of it will rub off on me."

Cheryl heaved a sigh. "So where will you be going?"

"They've already been out east, so after we leave here we'll be working our way up through California and into the northwest. We'll even have a few stops in Montana, Idaho and Wyoming before coming back through Utah and New Mexico. We finish in Austin. Stu said they'd pay for me to fly back and get someone to drive my car here."

"Huh. I've never been to any of those places, either. I must be getting old, because I'm not even jealous."

"Since your spectacular boyfriend lives here, I'm not surprised."

Cheryl's smile could have lit up the city. "You haven't said what band it is. Have I heard of them?"

"I hadn't. Jesse Rhodes is the songwriter and lead singer and he's got a backing band. A few of his songs are getting a lot of play right now," Beth said. She stood up and grabbed her laptop. "They're looking for his new album to do big things," she said, typing his name into a search.

"Jesse Rhodes. That sounds kind of familiar."

"I was so excited about the idea of traveling, I never even checked out his music. Let's hope I don't hate it."

"He's got a Wikipedia page," Cheryl said, pointing to the screen. "Click on that."

It wasn't much, just a paragraph with his basic bio and a description of his music as Americana and alt-rock. "Scorpion Dreams" was his third album. He was twenty-nine and born in West Texas. Back on the search page she clicked on one of the videos that popped up. Some appeared to be concert footage, others were of him playing at a radio station.

"Try that one," Cheryl said, pointing to one of him sitting in a studio, a wall of tapes behind him.

They were silent as Jesse started to play acoustic guitar, his gravelly voice clawing its way out of his throat as he sang a ballad about growing up in the desert, dreaming of snakes and scorpions.

He wore a cowboy hat, black jeans and a dark blue western-style shirt. The hat partially hid his face, but they could see enough.

"He's seriously hot," Cheryl breathed, leaning closer to the screen. "I like the song, too," she said, almost as an afterthought.

"Stu made me swear not to sleep with the band. If only he knew me."

"I don't know. Even a nice girl like you might want to drop her panties for this guy. I mean, look at him. And that voice."

"I can see that he's hot, I'm just saying that's not the kind of guy I would go for. I'm off *all* men right now. The last guy I'd ever sleep with is some semi-famous musician who probably sleeps with a different woman every night. I mean, please."

"You could enjoy looking at him, though. Nothing wrong with that." Cheryl looked back down at the screen. "Can we watch another one?"

***

The next day at ten minutes before noon Beth drove to the Holiday Inn and parked next to a white van, as Stu had instructed. She was early, though, and there was no sign of Stu or anyone else that might be in the band, so she sat in her car with the engine running and the air conditioner doing its thing. She was still getting used to the fact that even in early October the temperature hit the eighties in Las Vegas.

Her phone rang as she was sitting there staring off into space and she looked at it in dismay. Her mother. No way could she tell Deborah Levine that her twenty-eight-year-old daughter was running off with a band. Her mom was upset enough that she'd left their hometown of Gulliver, Ohio, for Sin City. This would send her over the edge.

She ignored the call and tried to ignore the surge of guilt at the thought of essentially lying to her parents for the next month.

Her stomach was turning itself inside out as the reality of what she'd signed up for sank in. What had she been thinking? Surely there were other ways to find adventure. She couldn't even remember the last time she saw a band live, and now she was supposed to help *run* one?

She was so immersed in her doubts she didn't realize anyone had shown up until there was a knock on her window. She gave a stifled yelp, feeling like a fool as she looked up at what had to be the sexiest man she'd ever laid eyes on.

Jesse Rhodes, in the flesh.

Dark, mussed hair under a beat-up cowboy hat, dark eyes bright with amusement, and a smile that could have curled a nun's toes. And she was no nun.

"Hey, honey. You waiting for us?" he asked, his deep, raspy drawl like a match against sandpaper.

Hearing it through her laptop's tinny speakers had been enough to spark discussion of panty-dropping, and it was nothing compared to the real thing.

The real thing coming out of the real man.

Her gaze dropped, unable to hold those laughing eyes, and she found herself looking at a tattoo of a rattlesnake coiled around each finely muscled forearm. They were artful, almost delicate, the black ink shading lighter and darker in a realistic diamond pattern.

Here were the snakes, just like in the song. Would there be scorpions inked onto the lean muscles hiding under that t-shirt of his?

This man was too good-looking, too sure of himself. She could feel the pull of him through glass and metal. He seemed to be waiting for her to get out of the car, or at least roll down the window.

Part of her wanted to remain in the safety of the car, maybe even drive away and forget the whole thing. Then she pictured the alternative – sitting in a cubicle at another accounting firm without having tried anything new – and she got out of the car.

Heat billowed up from the parking lot's freshly tarred surface, and instantly she was drenched in sweat. Jesse stepped back and looked her up and down without even trying to hide it. His smile widened.

Maybe she should have worn something else. Like a potato sack. Her sporty aqua tank dress wasn't cut low or overtly sexy, but standing next to this man she was suddenly aware how much of her skin was on view.

"You must be Beth," he said, holding out his hand.

It was a big hand. She took it, hating how aware she was of everything about him. She was tall, but he had her by several inches. It was more than that, though. Even in a t-shirt, cargo shorts and running shoes the man had presence. No wonder he was making a name for himself.

"You must be Jesse," she said, shaking his hand in a firm, business-like way, hoping to make a point.

"That's a real firm handshake you got, Beth," he said, his eyes teasing.

Could he read her so easily? How mortifying.

Another man came out of the hotel, one she recognized from his Facebook profile. He was a touch shorter than her with a narrow face and deep-set eyes that seemed to bore into her. Where Jesse was tanned, Will was pale, and his skinny frame showed the beginnings of a gut over his plaid old-man shorts.

She gave herself a mental shake for comparing the two men.

"Hi, Will," she said, pulling her hand from Jesse's and giving it to the other man. "Thanks so much for all your help."

"No problem. I was psyched when Stu told me he'd hired you."

Turning she saw Stu coming toward them, two men carrying duffle bags and guitar cases trailing behind him.

"That's Matt," Will said, gesturing toward a bearded guy with sleepy eyes and flip flops. Matt gave a genial grunt. "And that's Brian."

Brian was short, with dark curly hair and a serene smile. He was the only one wearing a wedding ring.

She'd come prepared, determined to prove Stu had made the right call. Opening her back door she pulled out a tray holding five iced coffees, then walked around the car and held them out.

Jesse grinned and took one. "Hell, Stu. If I'd known this is who you'd get for us, I'd have pushed Pete down the stairs myself weeks ago."

"Yeah, way to go, Stu," Matt echoed.

Stu snorted and unfolded a map across the floor of the van. Beth peered at it over his shoulder, her excitement spiking again as she saw their route through the desert.

Stu folded the map with a heavy sigh and looked at Beth. "Let's get the rest of this stuff loaded and head out. Santa Barbara's five hours away and I want to check into the hotel before we load-in at the club."

She'd already emptied everything from the car but her own bags and some extra water, but there was so much gear – duffel bags, guitars, an amp – that she had to put the back seats down as well. She turned around from wrestling with the seats to find everyone but Stu staring at her ass. Only Brian tried to hide it.

She scowled at them until they looked away. She felt messy and gross, her hair sticking to her forehead and neck, but you'd never know it the way these guys kept looking at her.

"I'll ride shotgun with Beth," Jesse said, stowing his bag and guitar case before closing the door with a slam.

"Wait a second, I was going to–" Will started to say, just as the other guys started debating who should ride with her.

Jesse turned to Beth. "You want me to drive first shift?"

"Um, no, I'll drive."

The other guys fell silent as it became obvious there was no point in arguing further. Jesse was the alpha dog here, no question, and it looked like she was going to spend the next five hours fending off his charm offensive. She glanced over at Will and caught the dark look he gave Jesse. There was something going on there, but there as no way to know if it was over being shouldered out of the way or something more.

Excited anticipation fizzed through her as she climbed into the car. Jesse got in on the other side and she pulled out, following Stu.

Jesse tossed his cowboy hat into the back and slid a pair of sunglasses on.

"If we're going to be driving together for the next four weeks we need to make sure we're compatible."

What did he mean by that? Did he intend to drive with her every time? She didn't ask. For now she'd just take things as they came. She'd probably need to be a little more relaxed on the road than she was in her normal life.

"May I?" he asked, picking up her iPod from where it sat between the seats.

She frowned at him, oddly defensive before he even looked. The last thing she needed was some judgmental artist to find her wanting. "I suppose."

"You can't know a person until you know what kind of music they like," he said, scrolling through.

"So you think you'll figure me out just by looking at my iPod?"

"Even I'm not that arrogant, but it's a good place to start. Your music is a window to your soul."

She wasn't sure she liked the sound of that, but let him look. They might as well figure out what they had in common so they could play some tunes for the road.

"Now this is interesting." He looked at her then back to the device. "Amy Winehouse, Ben Folds Five, Bob Dylan. Not bad, and I haven't even made it past the Bs."

"I'm so glad you approve."

He ignored her sarcasm and continued to scroll. "You like Gilliam Welch? I played with her at a festival last summer."

"Seriously?" she said, taking her eyes off the road to look at him.

"Abso-fucking-lutely. She was awesome. Dave Rawlings, her partner, is a master. I would love to tour with them."

"Hm. Too bad I wasn't with you last year."

"You would have hated it. This tour's way more civilized. We're still operating on a shoe-string, but the album's doing well and we've been able to upgrade to actual hotels. Last year it was either stay at some flea bag motel or on a friend's couch."

He was looking at her iPod again. "Justin Timberlake, huh? All the ladies like him."

"Jealous?" she asked, arching a brow at him.

He shrugged a shoulder. "Maybe a little. He's definitely got that something."

She refrained from telling him so did he.

"I've got something I think you'll like," he said, switching her iPod for his.

A few seconds later a song started playing, one that sounded vaguely familiar.

"I feel like I've heard it before, but I can't place it."

"This is Waylon Jennings, honey. Where I come from, he's practically a religion."

He flashed that smile again, the smile that shot straight to her stomach and down to her toes, stopping at every place in between. One of his front teeth was a little crooked, twisted so that one edge poked out a fraction beyond the other, and for some reason it struck her as a hundred times sexier than a perfect row of teeth.

She breathed a sigh of relief when he put his sunglasses back on, but he couldn't hide the rest of him. She could feel him studying her and resisted the urge to turn her head.

"Are you from Vegas?" he asked.

"No, Gulliver, Ohio. It's a small town south of Columbus. I just moved to Las Vegas a week ago."

"What for?"

She shrugged. "I needed a change and that's where my best friend lives. I've been in Ohio my whole life. Plus my parents are a little...not stifling exactly, but they're just so cautious, and I needed to get away from that."

"Huh, sounds a little like my parents."

"Most parents, really. I think it goes with the territory. It didn't help that my dad had a big set-back just a few years into their marriage. I think it's colored everything since."

"What happened?"

"He was laid off during the air traffic controllers strike in eighty-one. None of them were allowed to work again in that field so my dad had to start all over when he was thirty. I think that made them both risk-averse, as we say in the biz. They always encouraged me to do something practical so that I'd never have to worry."

"Right, Stu said you were an accountant. You can't more practical than that, can you? My parents would have loved if I'd done that. They wanted me to get out of our town as much as I did, but they were hoping I'd do it by going to college. My mom actually cried when I told her that was never going to happen."

"Because you wanted to play music?" she asked.

"Yeah, but I was never one for school. I was too restless and bored." He smiled at her. "Looks like we both ran away to be in a band."

"I guess I'm having my teenage rebellion a little late. Not that I've told my parents, mind you. It's bad enough I moved to Vegas. My mother would die if she knew I was doing this."

"I'm surprised Stu hired you. You don't seem like the type for this sort of gig."

"Why do you say that? Is it because I'm female?" she asked. She was only slightly annoyed. She *wasn't* the type, that was pretty obvious, but she wanted to hear what he thought.

"I guess that's partly it, but only because you don't get a lot of women doing what you're doing." He was serious now, the easy charm he'd been displaying since she met him falling away. "But it's mostly that you seem...nice. You're an upstanding citizen, not a semi-dirtbag like most people you meet on the road."

She couldn't help the face she made. "You make me sound so boring."

"You'd rather be a dirtbag?"

She huffed out a breath. "No, but I don't want 'up-standing citizen' to be the first thing that comes to mind when people meet me."

"Trust me when I say it's not."

She flushed, embarrassed and a little turned on by the implication behind what he said. He was attracted to her. She wasn't so clueless that she couldn't see that. But some guys came on to every woman they met. It didn't mean anything. And even if he didn't hit on everyone with a vagina, she wasn't going there.

"Touring's more exciting than an office job," he said, breaking into her thoughts, "but it's not exactly glamorous. I do it because it's part of the job, and in between the hours of driving and endless hotel rooms I get to go up on stage and play for people. It's a crazy high and I pretty much live for it. But you won't even get that."

"Are you trying to talk me out of this or something?" she asked.

"I just want you to know what you're getting yourself into."

"I know I want something totally different than what I've been doing. What would be the point in moving if I didn't try something new?"

"Fair enough."

Jesse pulled out a notebook and Beth turned her attention to the scenery. The side of the road was littered with scraps of twisted black rubber flung from truck tires, and everywhere she looked she saw dun-colored earth covered with some sort of scrubby bush.

Driving through it she felt more than ever that she was worlds away from her former life as an Ohio accountant, a woman on the verge of getting married. The landscape proved that more than anything with its alien contours and coloring, its terrifying heat just outside the shell of the car. Nothing looked or sounded or smelled like she was used to.

This was the adventure she was after, but as glad as she was to have made the leap, the sense of liberation she'd been waiting for wasn't coming. If anything she felt more unsure of herself.

What if the car overheated in the middle of this godforsaken place? There were hardly any cars out here. Already she'd gone miles without passing one. She had a couple of gallon jugs of emergency water stowed in the back seat, but even so, the thought of some unforeseen calamity worried at her.

She glanced over at Jesse. He was writing, his tangled hair hiding his eyes from her. Even as still as he was he radiated energy, and it was an uncomfortable and seductive thing.

Having him in the car felt dangerous, kind of like all that heat outside. She wasn't sure how to handle any of it and she was starting to realize she'd jumped into something she wasn't the slightest bit prepared for.

Chapter Two

Jesse looked up from his notebook to find Beth gripping the steering wheel with both hands, as if the car might suddenly bolt out of her control. They were in the middle of the Mojave desert with virtually no traffic, no cops in sight and she was going a steady sixty-five miles per hour like the good citizen she was. She nibbled on her bottom lip, frowning in concentration or worry.

"You okay?"

Her body jerked and she turned toward him. "What?"

"You seem a little tense. I was just wondering if you're okay. I 0 like."

"I'm fine, thanks," she said, defensive.

"Okay." He paused, trying to work out how to say what he wanted to say without pissing her off. She was on edge, though, so probably it wouldn't matter how careful he was. "It's just that you could go a little faster."

"But the speed limit is sixty-five. I don't want to get a ticket."

God she was adorable.

"Trust me, you won't. No one bothers with this stretch since it's more or less a death trap. The sooner human beings get out of it, the better."

"Oh. Okay."

She sounded doubtful, and she was biting her lip again as she depressed the gas. They were now going a whopping sixty-eight miles per hour. He had to hide his smile.

"Just out of curiosity, have you ever gotten a ticket?" he asked.

"No, never." She grimaced. "God, I'm boring."

"Maybe just more careful than you need to be."

Her mouth tightened and she only looked at him, clearly torn between her need to be good and her desire to break a rule. The speedometer crept up higher and her knuckles turned white as they car reached a cruising velocity of seventy-five.

"There you go, honey. Now just set the cruise control, sit back and enjoy the ride."

She did as he suggested and sagged back against the seat as if relieved the car had taken over. She really was wound kind of tight. Maybe his role in her little adventure would be to help her loosen up. If so, he was definitely up for the job. Her good girl vibe was seriously turning him on.

He'd thought she was pretty when he first saw her through her car window, but that was nothing compared to watching her unfold her long body from the car to stand at her full height. She was toned and curvy, like a pin-up girl, but with way more wariness in her wide hazel eyes.

There was something pure and innocent about her. He'd bet anything she'd been a good girl even as a teenager, the kind who would have babysat during high school and never ever snooped through the parents' drawers or had a boyfriend over after the kids went to sleep.

His body tightened at the way her short, caramel colored hair revealed her neck, and he pictured himself kissing his way down her throat and into the delicate fretwork of her collarbone.

Stu had warned them all away from her, but that didn't mean shit. Everyone knew bringing a woman on tour was a hazard. He'd already pissed Will off and it was probably gonna happen again. But it was his band, and he could handle Will.

"You hungry?" he asked, no longer content with the silence.

She glanced at him then back at the road, still vigilant. "A little. Why, do you have something?"

"I have a few morsels," he said, his teasing voice back again. It was pretty much automatic when he was talking to a pretty woman.

Rummaging around in his backpack, he came up with two unopened bags. "Barbecue potato chips, fried pork rinds or pretzels?"

"Pork rinds?" she asked, clearly disgusted.

"Nah, not really."

She gave him an exasperated look. "Pretzels, thanks."

He opened the bag and set it between them. "You want me to drive?" he asked.

"No, I'm good. Maybe in an hour or so."

She popped a pretzel into her mouth and chewed. He watched her tanned throat work as she swallowed. Shit, the woman even looked hot eating pretzels.

"So what's the story with your tattoos?" she asked. "Do they mean something, or are they just supposed to be cool?"

"You really want to know?" he asked.

"Obviously."

"I got bit by a rattlesnake. Twice."

"No way."

"Yup. Once when I was nine and again when I was sixteen."

"So the tattoos are, what, symbols of your near-death experiences?"

"As a matter of fact, yes, in a way, and I'd appreciate it if you didn't sound so skeptical. It hurts my feelings."

She snorted. "I doubt that."

She had him there.

"Rattlesnakes don't tend to kill people," he said, figuring it was only fair to admit that up front. "They can take out small animals and really young kids, but even at nine I was too big to die from it. Not that I knew that at the time. I thought I was done for. And I definitely could have lost part of my leg."

Beth turned down the radio. "Go on."

He had her now. This was a good story, so he'd give her the long version.

"We lived south of San Antonio, bordering on the desert, and there are a few different kinds of rattlers in those parts. I'd seen them before from a distance. They like to live in old buildings, and one day me and my buddy were prowling around an abandoned shack a few miles from home. I pulled a board away from the wall and bam, I got bit."

"What did you do?"

"Well, shit. I started to cry, of course. Told my friend Juan to go get my dad, then sat down on the ground, convinced I'd be dead before anyone came back for me. I saw my short life pass before my very eyes."

"So what happened?"

"Well, I lived, obviously."

Beth swatted his arm. "Come on, give me all the details."

"I started to feel sick, like all dizzy and nauseous, and then my dad was there, skidding to a stop near me in our shitty car. Juan was staring out the window, and I could see tears streaming down his face, too. He must have run like hell, and it was a couple miles back to our house." He was feeling oddly emotional remembering Juan's face and his own fear. He rubbed the spot where the snake had bit his wrist. "We were an hour away from the hospital and my dad held my hand the whole time and talked to me, asked me questions to take my mind off my fear, told me and Juan stories about when he was a kid."

"He sounds like a great dad."

Jesse smiled even as his heart contracted thinking about him. "He is. I gave him plenty of trouble, but he's a good man. Works way too hard with not too much to show for it."

She was quiet for a minute, as if sensing where his mood had gone.

"So what happened the second time?" Her voice was softer now, the teasing edge gone.

"I was making out with a girl named Maria on a pile of hay in a friend's barn and I felt something bite my ankle. I looked down and saw the snake slide away, but I knew from the first time that it wouldn't kill me, and we were closer to the hospital than I'd been before, so I didn't say anything."

"You got bit by a rattlesnake and you kept kissing a girl?"

"Hell, yeah. I wasn't sure I'd get another chance with Maria, and it was the first time I'd ever gotten to second base. I wasn't going to let go of her breast voluntarily, I can tell you that."

He could feel Maria even now. Her warm skin, the way she squirmed under him and breathed his name...

"Hello, Earth to Jesse." Beth was smirking at him like she knew where his thoughts had drifted.

"I did get a few more seconds of kissing out of it," he continued, "but then Maria saw the snake and screamed. It was pretty clear the making-out was over, so I told her I'd been bit, got in the car and drove myself to the hospital. Maria told her girlfriends about it and within a day everyone thought I was a total stud. Maria came back for more, too."

"You're shameless."

"Hey, I earned it."

Beth shook her head, but she was smiling.

"So in answer to your question," he went on, "the tattoos remind me that I can survive anything, no matter how scary it is." He examined the tattoo on his left arm, remembering the bite of the needle, how it had felt to open up to the pain. "They remind me that most things seem scarier than they really are. But they also remind me not to be a fool. Just because something won't kill you doesn't mean you should do it."

"Huh. That's quite a story," she said, sliding him a look. "Lucky for you, you were bit by something cool. You could have ended up with rabid skunk tattoos."

"You're a riot," he said, swallowing his laugh. Thank God he had a pretty healthy ego. This woman was not to be trifled with. "Any near-death experiences for you?" he asked.

"Not unless you count almost marrying my cheating ex-fiancé. That would have sucked the life right out of me."

Jesse looked at her, surprised by the turn the conversation had taken. She didn't look upset through, just distant and thoughtful.

"You mean if you'd stayed with him, knowing he'd cheated on you?"

"That was never an option. No, I mean even if everything had gone as planned, I'd have been unhappy. I was already frustrated. Marrying him was going to rule out all sorts of possibilities. I wanted to leave Ohio some day, and he refused to consider it. When I talked about going back to school he argued against it, even though I'd helped support him through med school. It was nothing awful, just sort of ...I don't know, like all the doors were slamming shut on me." She sighed and gave a rueful smile. "I convinced myself I was over-thinking it, and that all couples make compromises. But looking back, I can see I was the only one compromising."

"I guess you dodged a bullet then," he offered.

She smiled and looked out the window, settling deeper into the seat. "I guess I did."

They drove for a while without talking, the music filling the air between them. He jotted down ideas for songs – words and phrases, chord progressions – but remained completely aware of her.

He glanced up when Beth started to hum along with Shania Twain. She seemed lost in thought, maybe even unaware of what she was doing, and soon she was quietly singing along. He said nothing, afraid she'd stop if he called attention to it. He just let her sing them down the long stretch of highway, amazed at how fast the time flew with her.

***

Beth let Jesse drive the last stretch and almost immediately regretted it. It was only her squeal of protest when he hit ninety miles an hour that made him slow down to a semi-civilized eighty. She tried to relax and let the motion of the car lull her as it usually did. It worked, sort of, but mostly she was too aware of Jesse. Jesse and those sinuous snake tattoos winding around his truly fabulous forearms. They would have overpowered most men, but Jesse had enough charisma that they served him rather than the other way around.

Lucky little Maria, kissing Jesse in the hay. She was even commemorated in a way by the tattoos.

It was ridiculous, but she was actually turned on by the idea that he'd kept on kissing that girl even after being bitten by a rattlesnake. Even the playful attention he'd paid her so far had her entire body humming. Imagine being with a man who thought kissing you was more important than anything, even toxic venom coursing through his body.

But maybe he wasn't like that anymore. Women were probably a dime a dozen for him now.

It was almost a relief when they arrived at the hotel, though it meant she was actually going to have to start working and she had no clue what that really meant.

Grabbing her bags she followed him from the car, her gaze moving from his corded arms to his tight ass, only to be brought up short when she ran into him. He stood there holding the door for her and grinning as she blushed red hot and passed by him without a word.

The rest of the band arrived just as she and Jesse finished checking in.

"Jesse has a radio spot at five-thirty across town," Stu said. He looked tired from the drive but was no less intense for it. "I've got contracts to look over, so I want you to take him," he said to Beth. "You'll need to leave in," he looked at his watch, "twenty minutes. Give the DJ these talking points and make sure he mentions the California shows and new album. Go straight to the club afterwards for load-in and soundcheck."

"Oh, okay," she said, trying not to look rattled as she took down the instructions on a pad of paper she had in her purse.

The guys were already heading for their rooms.

"Got that, Jesse?" Stu called. "Meet Beth here in twenty minutes."

"Got it, chief," Jesse said, his guitar banging against his leg as he turned the corner and disappeared.

Stu turned to her. "You good?" he asked.

She nodded and he walked off without another word, looking at his phone.

This wasn't how she liked to do things. She worked best with everything planned out in advance. Back home she had lists and schedules and excel spreadsheets. Going with the flow was not working for her. She'd have to get a copy of their itinerary from Stu so that she wasn't taken by surprise every step of the way.

She looked around the lobby, its worn maroon carpet and threadbare chairs typical for a lower-priced chain, but better than the kind of dirt cheap motels she'd feared. Her room was standard fare, nothing fancy but clean and air-conditioned.

She'd had her phone off all day so that nothing would distract her or annoy her new employers on her first day, so she threw her bags down and checked her messages. One message from Cheryl, one from her mother. She called Cheryl first.

"Good, you're still alive," her friend said.

"Not that much has happened yet, just a lot of driving, but I'm getting to know Jesse better. He seems decent. Kind of cocky, but nice."

"You drove five hours with the hot lead singer? Yikes."

Beth laughed and flopped onto the bed. "It wasn't like that." She thought for a second. "Well, maybe it was a tiny bit like that, but only because he's pretty flirtatious. He's like a whole different species from Jeff. Which is pretty refreshing, I have to say."

"Refreshing enough to cut your man moratorium short?" Cheryl teased.

"No way. He probably flirts with everyone."

"Well, they definitely picked the right woman for the job. You'll have that band whipped into shape in no time, and you won't take crap from anyone. At least, I hope you won't. Make sure they treat you right."

Beth laughed. "Don't worry, I'll be fine." She looked at her watch. "Damn, I've gotta go. We're leaving in fifteen minutes and I still have to call my mom and shower."

"Call me soon, okay?"

She agreed, smiling as she hung up. Weird how their roles had reversed. For years she was the one worrying about Cheryl, scared that she was going down a dark road with the strip club and bad boyfriends. Now Cheryl was the settled one, the one whose life was on course.

It was silly to compare, though, and anyway, it wasn't like she was tragically lost or something. She was just going through a transition. Change was healthy.

She took the quickest shower of her life, glad all over again for her shorter hair. Jeff had liked it long so she'd left it like that for him despite her desire for a change, but the week after they split up she'd had it cut. It had been ridiculously liberating to feel all that hair falling away like so much baggage. Like she was cutting Jeff out of her heart and her life, becoming the person she'd been wanting to be.

Now it fell to her chin in shiny layers, and she couldn't help but think it made her look younger and more carefree. Like the kind of person who might have fun or take a risk now and then.

Still dripping on the carpet she called her mom while tearing through her clothes. Luckily her mom didn't pick up and she could make it a quick and easy message, one that gave no hint she was living a mother's worst nightmare.

Opening her suitcase she scanned through her tank tops, t-shirts, jeans and skirts. What did assistant road managers generally wear to Americana/rock/country shows? Then again, it didn't really matter what people usually wore, because she was unlikely to have it. She had the most boring wardrobe ever, though maybe that was just as well since she wasn't looking for anyone to notice her.

That decided, she pulled on a plain black t-shirt and denim skirt.

Time to go. She put on more deodorant, smoothed some tinted balm over her lips, grabbed her tote bag and rushed out the door.

She stood around for several minutes, already starting to sweat from nerves, and was just beginning to worry she'd have to go looking for Jesse when he sauntered into the lobby in jeans and a t-shirt, his guitar and messenger bag slung across his shoulders. His gaze took her in from top to bottom, and judging from his lopsided grin, he was perfectly happy with her sartorial choice.

"So why are you the only one getting interviewed?" she asked once they were en route. "Shouldn't the whole band come along?"

Jesse sighed and ran his hands through his hair. From the looks of it, she'd worried more about her appearance than he had.

"Well, I write everything. I mean, they contribute obviously, but they're my songs. Plus sometimes I need other musicians. I've been playing with Matt and Brian for years, though, and we're pretty tight. They get some decent paychecks working with me, but they also work with other musicians in between gigs."

"So Will's new?"

"Yeah. The guy who was supposed to tour with us backed out at the last minute when his wife got sick, and Will was available. I'd never met him before, but Stu knew him."

He sighed and leaned his head against the seat, his eyes closing.

Now that she looked, she could see he was tired. Dark circles shadowed his eyes and the electric energy he'd emitted the whole way to town had worn off. Now he was just a guy who'd been up late for a lot of nights in a row.

She was looking forward to the show tonight, looking forward to seeing what the band could do with an audience in front of them. From what she'd seen on YouTube they put on a good show, but she already knew that seeing Jesse in person and seeing him on a little screen were two entirely different things.

Her Australian GPS guide, whom she referred to as "mate" whenever she talked to him in private, guided them into the radio station parking lot with a few minutes to spare. Jesse grabbed his guitar and cowboy hat and started for the glass doors.

Beth stopped him with a hand on his arm.

"Are they going to be recording video of this?" she asked.

"I think so."

"Then lose the hat," she said, moving to take it from.

He clutched it to his chest. "What for? This is my lucky hat."

"It'll hide your fabulous face and hair. Give the ladies something to look at."

"Seriously?"

"I'm the assistant road manager. I know what I'm talking about here."

He shook his head, a wry smile curling that fine mouth of his. "Whatever you say Miz...what's your last name?"

"Levine."

His smile went from wry to dazzling. "Mm. A nice Jewish girl."

She grabbed the hat and swatted him with it before throwing it in the car. "Not that nice. Let's go, cowboy."

Once inside she handed the DJ the sheet of information and Jesse was ushered into the studio. She sat in a tiny room that seemed to function as a lobby, though it had just a few scattered chairs and a spring water dispenser. It also had a window into the studio so she could see and hear Jesse and the DJ chatting while a guy adjusted a video camera and the sound engineers did their thing. Then the recording sign lit up and the DJ introduced Jesse to his listeners.

"Tell us about playing with Buddy Higgins," the DJ began. "You started with him pretty young from what I hear."

"You heard right. When I was seventeen the band I was in opened for him in Austin. After our set he told me he'd liked what he heard and asked if I wanted to play guitar for him."

"Pretty impressive for a kid that young."

"Yeah. He'd fallen on hard times but he still had his chops. My parents were totally against it, but in reality they were never around to stop me. I mean, I was hardly home and they were always working, so I just kind of did what I wanted. It was pretty crazy because we played a lot of roadhouses, just a lot of dives in general, and they could get kind of rough. I learned a hell of a lot playing with him."

"You played covers when you first went out on your own, if I'm not mistaken. When did you start writing your own songs?"

"As soon as I started to play, but early on I was really just copying the music I liked. It wasn't until I was maybe nineteen or so that I started to develop my own sound. It was a few years more before I wrote something that wasn't derivative or just plain awful."

"I hear a little bit of everything in your music," the DJ said. "Some old school country, some blues, rock."

"I like so many different artists and genres, I guess it all just comes through."

"That it does, and we're thrilled to have you in our neck of the woods. Why don't you give us a taste of what we'll hear tonight at the Granada."

"Glad to," Jesse said, digging in his pocket for a pick. "'Course, I'll have the band behind me, but this'll give an idea. This one's called 'Waiting for the Rain' and it's on the new album, 'Scorpion King.'"

Then he started to sing, and even sitting in a soulless, over-air conditioned room, his voice slayed her. The song he'd chosen was mournful and yet had hints of light in it that made it somehow uplifting. Or maybe it was uplifting the way anything beautiful was, whether it made you laugh or cry.

She'd been right about leaving his hat off. Being able to see his face, to see when he closed his eyes as he sang, lent a greater intimacy to his playing.

He was talented, and the realization chased away her lingering doubts about coming on tour. Until two days ago she'd never heard of Jesse Rhodes, but he was the real thing. She'd be putting her efforts into someone who deserved to be heard, who'd make people feel something. It was a far cry from the world of accounting.

The DJ asked him more questions about the album and Jesse played another song, this one an upbeat, rocking little number that had her tapping her toe. He didn't look tired anymore. His energy was back, full but sort of throttled back for the intimate surroundings. Still, she couldn't take her eyes off him. The guy was charismatic, a star waiting to be discovered.

"That was really good," Beth told him once they were back in the car.

"You think?"

She looked at him, surprised by his apparent need for reassurance. "You sounded great. Couldn't you tell?"

He shrugged. "It's weird playing like that. You're not alone, but you don't have the energy of an audience to work off either."

"Well, I was sold," she said, his uncertainty making her want to reassure him. It was the truth anyway. "If I wasn't already going to your show, I'd want to now."

He gave a little smile, the tension leaving his shoulders.

"That first song was so sad. Is it about your father?"

"Inspired by him, I guess you could say."

For a second she thought that was all he was going to tell her. He picked up his hat and rubbed his thumb along at the curled edges like it required all his concentration.

"My dad's a mechanic," he finally said. "A good one, and my mom works as an aide in a home for seniors. There's hardly any work so they do what they can. I respect the hell out of them, but I've never understood why they didn't leave town when they were younger." He put the hat on, then took it off again, a frown between his brows.

"When I was younger I was mad all the time that I had to live someplace that seemed like such a dead end. I get kind of crazy when I think what it must be like for my dad. I suppose I identify with him, and it seems like such a waste to work so hard for so little."

"Do you think he hates his life?"

He thought for a second. "Actually, he's always seemed pretty content with what he has. That's part of what drives me crazy. I would hate to be that invisible. Like nothing you say or want matters to anyone."

"Maybe he's okay with what he has, though. Who knows, if your parents love each other..."

"So you're saying I shouldn't be upset by how they live?" he asked.

"God, I don't know. I don't blame you for wishing they had easier lives. People often settle for too little. I guess I just mean that maybe they're okay."

He seemed to take this in. "Maybe you're right. I mean, they're appalled by how I live, too. But I send them any money I can spare, and someday they'll have a decent place to live, even if it's in the same shitty little town.

"Well, there you go. Everyone'll be happy."

He gave her a funny smile, like he wasn't sure whether he believed it but really wanted to.

Matt, Brian and Will were unloading gear when she pulled into the Granada parking lot and up to the back door. She caught the guys ogling her as she and Jesse unloaded the car, and Jesse scowled at them like he was the only one allowed to stare at her ass. She ignored them all, glad to move after all the driving they'd done.

Stu was waiting for her when she returned from parking the car. "Here, put this on," he said, shoving a shirt at her. "You'll handle the merch table."

"Um, what's a merch table?"

He didn't even bother to sigh. "Merchandise table. We're selling CDs and t-shirts and a few vinyl pressings. The price list is in the box," he said, pointing to the boxes she'd just brought in. "Set up opposite the bar, and whatever you do, don't let one of the club staff take over the table. I told that shithead there was no way, but if someone comes over, you get me. You'd think taking a thirty percent cut would make them happy, but they're always looking for ways to screw us."

"Why do you let them take such a big cut of the stuff you sell?"

"That's the industry for you. They take a huge cut of the door and they take as much as they can of our merchandise sales. I'm hoping we can get better terms once we hire a business manager. I've been handling all the contracts, and frankly I don't have the time to haggle over each one."

"Does that mean you won't be Jesse's manager anymore?"

"It means I won't have to handle every damn thing myself. A business manager can handle contracts with clubs, insurance, and the financials. We'll need someone doing that after this tour so I have time to focus on his career." He sighed and looked around, his expression distant, like he was looking into the future. "I won't be touring with him anymore, either. We can get a tour manager for that. I'm too old for this shit anyway," he muttered, walking away.

Beth held up the shirt Stu had given her. Jesse's name was scrawled across the top in a slanting white font on the black background, and there was a photo of Jesse beneath that. It was the same image that appeared on the all the tour posters, sexy and brooding. A good likeness, though it had none of the humor she'd seen in him.

Given that she was a 34D, the medium he'd given her was probably the safest bet. She headed into the bathroom where she fussed with her hair before changing into the shirt. The fit was good, sexy rather than baggy, but without the annoying pull over her boobs. Unfortunately, now she had Jesse's face plastered to her body, and that was more than a little weird.

She passed Will and Matt as she headed back toward the boxes. Everything still needed to be brought into the main hall and put out, and she had no idea how long it would take her to get it all ready.

"Now *that's* an advertisement," one of them laughed behind her. "I only wish it was my face on that rack."

Burning with anger and mortification she turned around to see which of them had said it. Matt looked away like a guilty man, while Will just looked embarrassed.

Jesse was a few feet behind them, and when she caught the look on his face it was obvious he'd heard it, too. Before she had a chance to say anything, Jesse was in Matt's face.

"Apologize, asshole."

"I was just making a comment. I didn't mean for her to hear."

"Well, she did hear. Apologize or you're fined five hundred dollars."

"Are you shitting me?"

"Do I look like I'm shitting you?" Jesse growled. "Beth is saving our asses taking this job, which means we treat her with respect. Got that, asshole?"

Beth stood there, miserable. She'd never confronted any of the idiots who'd made comments about her breasts before. Usually she was too mortified, too meek to say anything. Besides, who wanted to confront the kind of jerk who'd say that? But she had to work with Matt and she couldn't let this set the tone for the next four weeks. Nor did she want Jesse fighting her battles for her.

She walked up to Matt and stood in front of him. "Forget the apology. I only want one if you mean it. I'll just point out that from this angle you appear to have a tiny dick."

Matt's mouth fell open in surprise. Will started coughing and Jesse stared at her in surprise before a pleased smile spread over his face.

"Now that we've both pointed out the obvious," she continued, a beautiful blast of confidence surging through her, "how about we move on?"

Matt colored but stood up. "It was a dumb thing to say," he muttered. "I didn't think you'd hear it." He wasn't quite looking her in the eye, but he seemed to be trying to. "You want a beer?"

She found herself smiling. "Sure, that'd be great."

Matt left and Will smiled at her, shaking his head in admiration. "Damn, that was stone cold, sister. Well played."

"It was pretty awesome," she acknowledged, unable suppress a huge grin.

Normally she thought of perfect put-downs long after an incident had passed. But she'd *killed* it this time.

Will's smile was open and friendly, with maybe just a hint of something more than friendliness. He was still shaking his head as he wandered off in the same direction as Matt.

"You didn't have to do that," Jesse said. "It's my band, my responsibility."

"I get that, but I can handle myself, and I don't want to be the reason you guys are snarling at each other. It'll only prove Stu's theory that he shouldn't have hired me. Besides, I need them all to respect me if we're going to work together."

He looked like he was going to argue, then just sighed and sat down on an amp and pulled his guitar onto his lap.

"I see your point, but that doesn't mean I'm going to stand around and let some guy give you a hard time. I'm not made that way."

She watched as he took off a broken string and began working a new one on. His hands were beautiful, big and strong, with long, mobile fingers.

"Is this some Texas cowboy thing?"

He looked at her then, his hands paused over the shiny, curving wood of his instrument. "No, it's a man thing."

Her heart jumped into her throat, her face flushing with sudden awareness. Her whole body lit with it, her nipples hardening under the t-shirt that *had his face on it*. Jesse's gaze stayed on hers for a long moment before he looked back down at the string in his hands.

Grabbing as many boxes of merchandise as she could hold, she hurried away, anxious to put as much distance as possible between them.

Chapter Three

The opening band started to load in and Jesse greeted them and made small talk before clearing out of the way. He was getting amped now, the sizzle he felt before every show taking hold. Not quite the adrenaline that kicked in when he walked on stage, but a lower-level hum that made him feel awake and alive.

Kind of like how he felt a few minutes ago with Beth.

He'd barely been able look at her as she stood over him blazing with heat, her nipples hard under her top. A top with his own damned face on it. It was all he could do not to stare at her incredible rack, but seeing as how they'd been talking about respect, that would've been pretty low. Besides, the look on her face was even sexier.

Her mouth was insane, full and wide and set in a face that was striking and kind at the same time. Her hazel eyes had a tendency to look either innocent or wary, and her wide mouth turned into a killer smile that softened her strong cheekbones. He couldn't remember meeting a woman with a cleft in her chin, but Beth had one, softer and more subtle than what a man would have, and for some reason it just about drove him crazy. He pictured himself holding her chin, his thumb nestled right in that little hollow, before he kissed her senseless.

"Hey, Jesse, get out here," Stu called from the stage, snapping him out of his reverie.

Jesse shook his head, smiling ruefully to himself. As tempting as it would be to get his hands on her, he probably ought to stick to the women who threw themselves at him every night. Things were a lot less complicated with women like that.

Usually soundcheck took no more than half an hour, but the sound guy, an obvious stoner named Kevin, didn't get what Jesse was after. His levels were all wrong and he didn't even hear it.

"Dude, this sounds like shit," Jesse said into his microphone. "Bring the guitars up and the drums down."

Kevin nodded and the band once again kicked into their first song, but now the guy had turned the guitars up so far Jesse couldn't hear Brian at all. Next tour he was bringing his own guy. Enough of this amateur hour bullshit.

"I'll handle this," Stu said, shooting him a quelling look.

Jesse waited while Stu went down to the soundboard and the two of them dicked around so long he just about lost it. The only thing that kept him from biting off everyone's head was the sight of Beth over at the merch table. She held a stack of CDs as she watched them, her mouth a tight, anxious line.

Stu gave the nod and they played bits and pieces of other songs, finally moving to an acoustic number he was thinking of doing that night. He couldn't even hear himself, and it didn't look like anyone else could either, but he was halfway through the song before the sound was adjusted correctly.

"That's enough," he said into the mic. He wanted to make sure Kevin heard him loud and clear. "Stu's handling my set tonight."

That got Kevin's attention. "Dude, what the fuck?"

Jesse ignored him. Putting his guitar on its stand he turned around and walked off stage. Luckily the table in the green room had a plate of sandwiches and barbequed ribs. Cracking open a beer, he threw a plate of food together and sat on one of the battered armchairs to go over the night's set list.

He scratched things out and re-ordered some songs as the rest of the band filtered back in. Beth came in a few minutes later and grabbed some food and a bottle of water. He watched as she scanned the seating options as if trying to decide whether she should sit near him. Did she think he was going to bite?

With forced casualness she finally sat down next to him, which was a relief since he didn't feel like talking to anyone else. She was a breath of fresh air after two months on tour with the same guys night after night.

He raised an eyebrow in acknowledgement and pretended to work on the set list. Really he was watching her eat out of the corner of his eye.

"God, I needed that," she said, coming up for air. A pile of rib bones lay on her plate. "Do you guys eat like this every night?" she asked, licking sauce off her fingers.

He watched her pink tongue dart in and out, watched her suck the tip of her thumb, completely oblivious to what she was doing to him. It was so innocent, like some kind of Ohio girl porn.

"We have riders in our contracts for food, but we only get it if the club we're playing has a kitchen. Otherwise we have to find something nearby."

She took another long drink of water and he watched her throat work.

"You seemed kind of harsh with the guy out there," she finally said.

"Maybe, but the last thing I need is to go on tonight worrying that idiot is going to screw up the sound. There are five hundred people who bought tickets for tonight's show, and I need to blow their minds. I can't worry about hurting his feelings."

She seemed to think that over, but she didn't look convinced.

"Are you one of those people who wants everyone to like her?" he asked.

"What? No."

He gave her a look.

"Maybe," she mumbled. "But I can't help it. I don't want people to feel bad."

"I'm not saying it's okay if I'm a dick to everyone who annoys me. And yeah, maybe I could have been less harsh with Kevin, but sometimes you can't worry about what's nice."

"I guess. Sometimes it's like I can't even admit I'm angry or hurt, you know?" she said, looking down at her plate. "You should have seen how calm I was when I found Jeff cheating on me."

"Seriously?" he said, amazed at the idea that a woman could be calm under those circumstances. In his experience, women generally screamed and threw things when they felt wronged.

"It's not like I was *happy* about it," she said, her eyes snapping, voice defensive. She grimaced. "Sorry, I shouldn't take it out on you."

"See, right there," Jesse said, pointing his beer at her. "Don't apologize. I'm being nosy and judging you. You should be pissed."

She gave a half-hearted laugh. "It's not like I didn't do anything," she said, frowning, her eyes on her hands. "I stopped by our house on my lunch break to get some paperwork for my new car, and I found him in the kitchen with her. They were half dressed and it was obvious what they'd been doing. It was a total cliché. He said it wasn't what it looked like, but I was just... I don't know, numb I guess. And I just thought, well that's it then. It's over."

She looked up, the remembered bleakness in her eyes enough to make his chest go tight. "I said something like 'I can't believe you'd do this' and he said it didn't mean anything. Meanwhile this woman in a t-shirt and underwear is still standing in my kitchen, holding a yogurt like maybe she's going to finish it. I told her to get out, and then I told him to move his stuff out while I was at work. But I didn't yell. Not once."

"Actually, that sounds pretty classy," he said. "Kind of like he wasn't worth wasting your energy on."

She smiled, though her heart wasn't in it. "I think... I think under the hurt and betrayal I was maybe relieved to have a way out. What he did was so clearly wrong, you know? It was clear-cut, unlike the doubts I'd been having."

"I can see that. Anyway, you're not a completely lost cause. You gave it to Matt pretty good back there."

She straightened up at that. "You're right. That was pretty badass. Maybe I've turned over a new leaf."

He grinned, glad to see her coming back to life. "A badass new leaf."

She laughed and tapped her water bottle with his beer. "I'll drink to that."

*****

Beth held Jesse's smile, warmth spreading through her at the idea of herself as classy and strong, not to be trifled with. Then guys from Chain Gang, the opening band, came into the room and piled into the seats all around them and their conversation was overtaken by other talk. A bong was filled and passed around to a chorus of coughing fits.

Beth got up to refill her plate, and this time she grabbed a beer. So what if she was working? This was a different world with different rules. Besides, she was a badass.

She was standing by a plate of cookies when Stu came over with a list of hotels she needed to call to confirm their reservations for the next week.

She took the list from him. "Do you have the schedule for the rest of the tour, and maybe something that shows all the interviews Jesse's booked for? I'd really like to see the whole picture. I work better that way," she explained.

He was silent for several seconds, during which she was convinced he was going to ream her out for being so presumptuous.

"I knew there was a reason I hired you," he said, breaking into a rare smile. "I'll send you what I have."

"I have a laptop back at the hotel. You could email me the stuff and I'll keep it on there. I have accounting software, too," she went on, pressing her advantage. "If you'd like I could also keep track of expenses."

He thought for a second, then nodded. "I'm crap at that kind of stuff, so I will let you handle that, but I'll be checking it over."

"Of course."

It took her longer than she expected to make all the confirmation calls to the hotels, and a couple of them had too many or too few rooms booked, so she had to fix those. The club had was just letting people in when she got off the phone. Grabbing a couple more cookies she hurried down a short hallway that led from backstage to a side entrance into the main room.

She made it to the table just before her first customers appeared. Nervous now, she pulled out the price chart and lock box and pasted a smile on her face.

"God, he is so sexy," one twenty-something woman said to her friend as they stood looking at t-shirts. "You're going to die when he gets up there, especially if you can see his arms. He's got killer arms."

"Are you going to try to get backstage after the show?" the friend asked.

"You bet your ass, I am. I didn't the last time I saw him 'cause I was with Joe, but there's nothing to stop me tonight. What about you?"

Beth tried to keep her face expressionless during this conversation, but she couldn't help the sinking feeling she got listening to them. Both women were hot and dressed to show it off. She didn't know how things worked with the whole backstage thing, but she was going to find out soon enough. And if they did let women backstage, these two would be in.

Dear God, don't let it be her job to decide who got backstage. If she was going to encounter sex, drugs and rock 'n roll, she would prefer to do it a little at a time rather than all on the first night.

Fan number one bought a shirt.

"Did you want any of the CDs?" Beth asked, feeling like maybe she should push the products.

"I have all his albums," the woman replied, handing Beth a twenty.

Beth smiled and watched her walk away. She had no business, no reason, to feel jealousy or resentment or anything else, but the idea of Jesse sleeping with the woman knotted her stomach.

How dumb was that?

She made a few more sales as the band set up and then the lights dimmed and Chain Gang went into their first song. People seemed to like them well enough, and though their music didn't do all that much for her, she was happy just being in the middle of all that energy.

After their set music was once again piped through the speakers and for the next half hour she had a steady stream of customers. It didn't take long for her to realize that manning the merch table wasn't rocket science. She had a good head for numbers and was quick to make change, and it was fun meeting new people. Everyone was there to have a good time and excited about seeing Jesse. Standing at the table gave her a sense of the devoted following he had. Many of the people there had seen him before and some of them were even following him from city to city.

No wonder he'd pitched such a fit at Kevin.

The sense of anticipation grew and her last few sales were made quickly as the house lights dimmed again. Everyone got to their feet, hollering and clapping as Jesse came out, the rest of the band trailing behind him.

The noise and applause went through her, filling her up until the whole room felt like it was in her head, her heart, pumping through her blood. Without saying a word Jesse counted off and the band ripped into the first song, and from that moment until the end she couldn't look anywhere but at him.

Now she saw with her own eyes what she'd sensed on first meeting him. He was electric, fluid, self-possessed and almost unbearably sexy. Everything she'd seen in him before was there, only turned up. Like he dialed down his charisma when off stage so as not to blind everyone.

He seemed to feed off of the crowd's energy. Even she found herself lifted by it. Hundreds of people packed into a small space, all leaning toward the band, wanting more, wanting it never to end. She was dancing and cheering and sweating along with everyone else by the third song, no longer thinking of anything but how good he sounded. How good he looked.

She was as swept away as anyone else, and even on the edge of the crowd the heat of hundreds of people packed together and moving to the music was a physical thing. Being in the middle of all that energy sent a thrill through her, made her feel more alive than she'd felt in years.

They finished up the rowdy number they'd been playing and then dropped down to just Jesse's guitar. He strummed lightly, almost absently, as he surveyed the crowd.

"How y'all doin' tonight?" he asked.

Five hundred people whooped and hollered back. Jesse laughed.

"You catch that, boys?" he asked, turning to the band. He looked back out at the crowd and Beth waited, breathless, for what would come next. "So we've got the new album, which by the way we're selling here tonight. You can purchase it from the lovely Beth over at that table," he said, pointing toward her with a grin. "But now I'd like to play a tune that's a bit more personal."

The crowd quieted, waiting while he pulled a harmonica rig over his head and tuned his guitar. Then he started to play. It was just him now, the rest of the band listening along with the audience as Jesse started to sing, and the first words that came to her mind were *high lonesome*. She couldn't think where she'd heard the term before, but it that's what she felt listening to him sing alone up there to the hushed crowd.

Whereas the first few songs they'd played had been either raucous or had a fun rockabilly sound, this was spare and haunting. When he played the harmonica, it was like the wind whistling thorough a lonely landscape. As the lyrics unfolded it became clear the song was about the kind of lives people lead on the edge of the desert, whether that was literal or metaphorical.

His eyes closed for long stretches, then opened to reveal those dark eyes, holding the same mournfulness. The way the lights shone on him, she could see the gleam of sweat at his throat. He picked out the last few notes, trailing off until there was complete silence in the hall. Then the noise rose to a whole new pitch, as if they too were moved by what he'd shown them. The smile he gave was pleased, maybe even shy. Like he'd revealed something he wasn't entirely comfortable with yet.

He turned to the band, gave them a signal, and the crowd subsided again as a new song started, this one with the band behind him. It was sober and melodious, and after a few bars she realized it was a love song, but just as spare and lonely as the previous one in its own way.

She hadn't expected this. The only songs of his she knew were the few she'd listened to the day she got the job and the ones she heard at soundcheck. But they hadn't really played the songs at soundcheck, not all the way through for real, and they'd been marred by the starts and stops, bad sound and Jesse's anger.

But this. This was the kind of music that made you sit in your car until the song was over. The kind that pinned you down in your own memories or heartbreak. When the song ended she tore her gaze from Jesse and looked at the rapt faces of the people around her.

She tried to imagine how it felt to be up there, looking out at a room full of people you held in thrall. Judging from his face, it was a powerful thing. He looked lit up, like the force of the audience's love was powering him now.

They left the stage for intermission and she was swarmed by people. The t-shirts sold like crazy and she discovered in the process that there were shirts emblazoned with the album cover instead of Jesse's face. Thank goodness. She'd be wearing that one from now on. She also sold a bunch of CDs and a good number of stickers and got nearly everyone to sign up for the mailing list.

Jesse played a few more ballads in the second set, but otherwise the songs were either a rollicking blend of country and rock or driving, hard-bitten songs that Jesse sang with a fierce energy that came close to fury without ever quite going over. The other guys were good musicians, but Jesse was the star, no question.

They left the stage to a deafening roar that continued until they came back for an encore. When it was over Beth felt strangely wrung out, like she'd been the one up there on stage, playing her heart out.

She spent the next half hour selling to fans who looked as exhausted and radiant as she felt. The air conditioning had long since stopped cooling the room and she was sweating like crazy as people made purchases. Gradually the rush slowed to a trickle and then it was over, the doors closing to the public. She counted up the money, thrilled with how much better they'd done than she'd expected. Then she remembered she had to give the club thirty percent. Funny how the band's success already felt like her own.

"How'd we do?" Stu asked, peering down at the inventory sheet where she'd recorded the sale of each item.

"I have nothing to compare it too, but it was pretty busy," she said, stretching out her back. "We made over three thousand dollars."

"Not bad," he said. "Pete never managed to make the right change, so it was always off." He looked around, then back at her, his expression weary but seemingly pleased. "Go ahead and give Steve the club's cut and we'll get this stuff loaded."

The band had taken their gear away while she was making sales so there was nothing left on stage but wires and a couple microphone stands. She gave the envelope to Steve and then together she and Stu hauled the boxes into her car.

"Things are picking up," Stu said, shoving the last box into her wagon. "We'll need to get more shirts and CDs or we'll run out by Portland. I'll give you the ordering information tomorrow."

"I had no idea they were going to sound so good. I mean, I just wanted the job so I wasn't really thinking about that part of it, but he could really go places, couldn't he?"

"You bet your ass he could, and he will. That's what this is all about." He leaned against the car, looking thoughtful. "What you're feeling now is pretty much what I felt the first time I saw Jesse playing in a dive bar outside Houston. He was living in his car and playing every chance he could. I offered to manage him then and there. That was six years ago and we've been working our tails off to make it happen for him. He's got a good following now, but he's about to tip over into something bigger."

"Well, I'll do what I can to help," Beth said. She slammed the hatch closed and they headed back into the club. She could hear music coming from the room where they'd hung out before the show.

Beth followed Stu toward the party, wondering what happened next. Did she wait around and drive people home, or was it every man for himself now?

Stu headed straight for the cooler but Beth stood inside the door trying to take it all in. There were probably fifty people – staff from the club plus everyone connected to the two bands, and a lot of women. The two women she'd heard early in the night were there, and the one who'd been determined to get in was already talking to Jesse. He was talking to a couple other guys but one arm was draped across her shoulders and every so often he looked at her and smiled. Even from where Beth stood fifteen feet away she could see the promise it held.

It wasn't any of her business, but somehow it bummed her out anyway. *Please, don't make me drive them to the hotel.*

She grabbed herself a beer and took a sip, surveying the room. Stu looked deep in conversation with a guy from the other band and she was trying to decide whether she should intrude on their conversation when Will came up to her.

"Hey there. I was wondering where you were."

"I was just packing everything up. If merchandise sales are anything to go by, you guys were a big hit."

"Yeah, it was a good night. The whole tour's been good, but we've been picking up steam the last few weeks."

"Do you tour a lot?" she asked.

"Now and then, but this is the most successful one I've been on. I just moved to Austin this past year, so I don't know everyone on the scene yet, but I met Stu my first week in town when I sat in on a recording session for an album he was producing."

"Huh. I didn't know he did that," she said, intrigued.

"Sure, that's his bread and butter. Jesse's the only musician he actually manages. He's kind of a legend in Austin."

Brian wandered over looking serene as ever. He didn't say anything, just listened.

"It was so different seeing you guys in person," Beth said, leaning toward them as the volume in the room increased. "I watched a couple videos of Jesse right after I took the job, just so I knew what I was dealing with, but tonight's show blew my mind. I had no idea what to expect, but Jesse had us all eating out of the palm of his hand."

Evidently that was the wrong thing to say.

Will's smile fell away and his expression hardened, a muscle twitching in his jaw. "Yeah, Jesse seems to have that effect on people."

"You guys sounded great. Really tight," she went on, unnerved by his abrupt change in mood.

"Yeah, well, no one really cares what we do. We're just here to make Jesse look good," he said, swigging the rest of his beer. "You want another one?"

"Sure, that would be great," she said, just to get a breather from him.

She watched Will weave his way across the room and wondered what his deal was. Professional jealousy, or was it more personal?

"That went well," she muttered. She looked at Brian. "You don't say much, do you?"

Brian shrugged a shoulder. "Not unless I need to."

She was starting to think that might not be a bad policy, especially around Will. She was mulling this over when Jesse caught her eye across the room. He leaned down and said something to the girl under his arm before heading toward Beth.

Brian drifted away without another word.

"So what did you think? Can you stand another month of listening to us?" Jesse asked, grinning playfully.

"You know you sounded great."

He looked serious all of a sudden. "Knowing and believing are two different things. As strange as it may seem, I occasionally need some reassurance."

"Don't all the screaming fans count?"

"They certainly help, but unfortunately I have a bottomless need for it." He shrugged a shoulder. "Goes with the territory. Plus we need to kick ass through California. I've put a lot of time in touring here, even before I hooked up with Stu. We need to make this count."

"What else are you guys doing to spread the word?" she asked.

"What do you mean?"

"You know. Are you tweeting from the road, keeping your Facebook page updated, that sort of thing."

He made a face. "Hell, no. I can't stand that stuff. Neither can the other guys, and Stu doesn't know shit about it."

"Seriously? You don't do anything?"

"I've been touring non-stop for the last ten years of my life. That's how we're getting the word out," he said, clearly defensive. "That's how it's always been done."

She narrowed her eyes at him, wondering whether there was any point in arguing with him. But his jaw was set and he was clearly annoyed. No, no point. Besides, if he hated doing it, it wouldn't go over well.

"Then I'll do it, she said. "I'll set up a Facebook page and a Twitter account for the band."

"What part of–"

"I'll do it all," she said. "Just leave it to me."

"What happens when you leave and we don't have anyone else to do it?"

"Good question. I have no idea, but we'll come up with something. The important thing is to make the most of your tour now. You need to get the reviews and interviews out there."

He was looking at her with extreme skepticism.

"Trust me. It'll be good."

"Fine. Knock yourself out."

She smiled, pleased she'd found something she could contribute, something no one else was doing.

His eyes flicked downward, then back to her face. His voice was low when he spoke again, and he leaned in closer. "You can worry about Twitter. I'll monitor how sweaty you get. If the t-shirt is sticking to you by the end of the night, I'll know we've rocked."

She sucked in her breath and took a step back, feeling her face flush. She opened her mouth to make an angry retort, then stopped at the look in his eye. He wasn't mocking her, he was...*smoldering* at her.

She was still trying to think what to say when fan girl came over, her expression a mixture of uncertainty and determination.

"Hey, Jesse."

"Oh, hey," he said, looking down at her and back at Beth.

He hesitated, as if torn, but Beth just smiled at both of them and excused herself. Not in this life would she be vying for Jesse's attention.

Will came back with her beer, but luckily for her he was dragged away by a friend. She felt a bit looser after her second beer, loose enough to let Steve flirt with her while he told her about the music scene in California. She picked his brain about what other bands were doing promotion-wise and got some good ideas for things she could do for Jesse.

Around two o'clock the alcohol was nearly gone and the party started to die out. Brian sat on the couch alone, a half-filled cup of beer resting on his leg. His eyes drifted shut and then popped open like a little kid trying to stay awake at his parents' party.

Looking around she spotted Matt strumming his guitar in a corner while talking to a couple of guys from Chain Gang. Will was leaning against a wall with a tiny woman who appeared to be hanging on his every word.

"Hey, Stu," she said, catching the manager between conversations. "Do you need me for anything, or can I head back?"

"Yeah, go ahead and take off. Take Brian while you're at it."

Relief flooded her that she wasn't going to have to approach Jesse or Will. Brian's eyes flickered to life when she told him she was heading to the hotel. They drove the ten minutes to the hotel without speaking, the radio playing softly in the air between them.

By the time she pulled into the hotel Brian's head was canted to the side and he was snoring. She cut the engine and gently shook his shoulder. Finally he opened his eyes and sighed, and the two of them got out and headed into the hotel lobby, parting ways as they walked in opposite directions down the hallway.

"Sleep tight," he called, disappearing around the corner.

It was such a homey thing to say that she smiled to herself all the way back to her room. She showered quickly and fell into bed, her brain spinning with the stimuli of the whole night – the weird thrill of confronting Matt, of being in the middle of all that energy. Jesse defending her. Jesse on stage, bringing out something in her she hadn't expected him to reach.

She woke up the next morning from a dream about Jeff, but instead of the sense of betrayal and wasted time she usually felt after dreaming of him, she thought about the day ahead and hopped out of bed, too excited to sit still.

They weren't leaving for Santa Cruz until one o'clock, and Stu had secured late check-outs for all of them, which meant she had time to get started on the finances. She made herself a cup of coffee from the pot in the room, and opened her laptop. She checked her email and found Stu had been as good as his word. At three-thirty this morning he'd emailed her everything she'd asked for.

An hour later it felt like she was starting to get somewhere. Stu had been keeping track of expenses in a word document, which was cumbersome but at least reasonably clear. He seemed to be accurate as far as the figures went, but there were better tools available to him. Which was why she laboriously entered all the information into spreadsheets that would do all the work for them once they were set up.

She'd been at it for two hours when she realized she was lightheaded with hunger. Pulling on a pair of shorts and a tank top, she slipped her feet into flip flops and headed for the Dunkin' Donuts next door.

She was just placing her order when she heard a familiar voice behind her. Turning around, she saw Jesse standing at the back of the line with the girl from the night before. They stood next to each other without touching, but the girl kept glancing up at him when he wasn't looking.

Beth grabbed her coffee and the bag containing her egg sandwich and headed toward the door, pasting a pleasantly surprised look on her face when Jesse spotted her.

His smile wasn't forced. It bloomed naturally, as if he were delighted to see her. "Hey. You're up early."

She looked at her watch and saw it was after noon already. "Maybe in rock star time," she said, raising an eyebrow at him.

He just smirked back at her. "You remember Trish."

"Yes, nice to see you again," Beth said, smiling at her.

Trish gave her a wary smile and leaned toward Jesse. She had on make-up, though less than the night before, and last night's skimpy clothes. She looked vulnerable in the bright light of day, but maybe that was just Beth projecting. She'd never been a Trish, never slept with a guy she didn't know. How did it feel the next morning? You'd been as intimate as two people could be, but now it was over and you'd probably never see each other again. She couldn't imagine it, but maybe there was something to not letting sex be such a big deal.

As she walked back to the hotel she couldn't help wondering what that would be like. Was it everything Trish had hoped and expected? Was anything as good as you expected it to be? Jesse was just a guy, after all. But maybe Trish didn't care about any of that.

It must be nice to live in the moment without trying to account for everything. Unfortunately, she'd probably never know what that was like.

Chapter Four

Jesse entered the lobby to find Beth and Stu sitting side by side on the sagging couch, their heads together as they looked at the computer on Beth's lap.

"So it's all here," she was saying. "We still need to save receipts, but this way it's all tracked for us. It's made for small business owners, not professional accountants, so it's pretty intuitive. I saved it as a Google doc and shared it with you, so we both have access to it."

Stu grunted and folded his arms across his chest. "This'll be good."

Beth seemed to realize this was high praise coming from Stu. She lit up, her smile bringing a weird ache to Jesse's chest. She'd only worked for them for two days. How could she care so much already?

She was so engrossed she still hadn't noticed him.

"I'll get those press kits put together before the show tonight so I can mail them tomorrow," she continued. "After that I'll get to work on the social media sites."

"Better be careful, Stu," Jesse said, finally making himself known. He was unaccountably annoyed that she could remain oblivious to his presence for so long. "If she's too good we might not need you anymore."

It was one of his jokes that when he got Jesus Christ famous he'd drop Stu and hire someone new and shiny, but they both knew that would never happen. Six years ago Stu had wandered into the dingy bar he was playing and seen something in him. He'd dedicated himself to Jesse's career ever since, and that was that. Jesse would fire every member of the band ten times over before parting ways with Stu. When you found someone who believed in you like he did, there was no turning your back on him.

Beth shut down the computer and stowed it in its case. "I guess we'd better get going," she said, slinging it over her shoulder, then bending down to grab her other two bags.

He grabbed her suitcase along with his guitar and duffel bag and headed for the door.

"What are you...?" she started, giving up as he left the lobby and made for her car.

He was usually later than everyone else when it was time to leave town, but he'd made sure to show up earlier than usual. He wasn't letting anyone else ride with Beth. Pretty soon everyone would understand the rule and wouldn't even try.

As soon as she unlocked her car he tossed his stuff in the back and leaned against the car, effectively staking his claim.

"Not sick of my company yet, huh?" she asked, a little smile curling the corners of her mouth.

She seemed amused, but perplexed, too, like she couldn't imagine why he'd want to spend the four-hour drive to Santa Cruz with her. For a woman as pretty as she was, it was bizarre how unaware she was. But then, that was part of what he dug about her, too.

Beth left to get coffees and he watched her go before finally turning away. Brian and Matt staggered out a minute later followed by Will, who scowled for no apparent reason and climbed into the van without saying a word to anyone. But that was par for the course with him.

By the time Beth got back they were all ready to go. She passed out coffees to everyone and then headed for the driver's side door.

"I can drive," he said, holding his hand out for the keys. "It's only fair."

She hesitated and bit her luscious lower lip.

"I swear on my momma's grave I'll drive within ten miles of the speed limit and I'll use the turn signal even if there are no other cars around."

She huffed out a laugh and shook her head, but she gave in. "Fine, you drive," she said, handing him the keys. "I'll be in charge of tunes."

Beth took the music selection very seriously. So seriously in fact that he thought she might never pick a song.

"What about Neko Case?" she asked, frowning down at her iPod. "Or no. Maybe Ben Nichols."

This had been going on for ten minutes.

"Beth, honey, just play something. Anything."

"Okay, okay," she said, and finally music started to play.

They drove along in companionable silence, except he was feeling a little *too* companionable. He'd had perfectly decent sex just last night, nothing spectacular, but it should have taken the edge off. Even still he was getting a little crazy sitting next to Beth.

She was wearing a pair of blue shorts and a plain white top. There was nothing overtly sexy about it, but just the fact that he could see miles of golden skin and toned muscle made his dick twitch.

"Do you run?" he asked.

"Huh?"

He cleared his throat. "I was just wondering if you were a runner. You look really...strong."

"Oh. Um, no, not really. I run sometimes but I'm more of a swimmer. What about you?"

"I mountain bike when I can but that's about it. My lifestyle doesn't lend itself to the healthiest habits."

"I suppose not. But you get a pretty good workout on stage every night."

He just grunted. It was true, but sitting next to Beth, the picture of health and vitality, he felt like a gnarly vampire.

The album ended and Jesse suggested they try the radio.

"I suppose so," she said, looking dubious. "If you think we'll find anything good."

"I can't promise anything, but you can find some great new music through local stations, especially college radio," he said. "You can't be surprised if you only listen to your own music. Plus, I kind of like the idea that other people are hearing the same thing I am. It's more communal, like at a show."

"I never thought of it that way."

He listened for a second to each station before moving on, looking for that special something.

"Wait! Go back," she said. "I love that song."

"'Leather and Lace?'" he asked, turning back to the previous channel.

She didn't bother to answer, just started singing along with Stevie Nicks, then with Don Henley when his verse came.

"You're singing both parts," he laughed.

"I always do."

"Well, maybe before you didn't have anyone else, but this is a duet. You stick to her part."

"Fine," she grumbled, rolling her eyes.

The next beat she was singing along with Stevie, her voice carrying a similar husky quality.

Jesse listened to her finish her verse and then picked up his part. He sang it straight, not joking around like she probably expected him to. It was actually a pretty good song, though he'd never admit that to a guy. They blended perfectly, their voices playing off each other without effort. He liked how Beth sang without embellishing, letting the strong melody and her voice do the work.

"That was pretty good," she grinned at him when the song ended. "I didn't think you had it in you."

"I am a singer, you know."

"I know. I just figured you wouldn't go for that sort of thing."

Jesse shrugged. "I like a lot of different music. You won't find me belting out 'Desperado,' but I can get behind a good ballad."

"They were together for a while," Beth said, looking very serious. "I think that's why they sound so good. You can feel their chemistry."

He was feeling some chemistry, too, and it wasn't just between those two on the radio.

"Not many people know it, but Stevie Nicks wrote that song for Waylon Jennings," he said.

"Really?"

"He asked her to write a song with that title for him and his wife, Jessie Coulter. She was a singer, too. But by the time she'd finished it, it was looking like Waylon and Jessie would be splitting up, so she recorded the song with Henley."

"Huh. I wonder what it would have sounded like if Waylon Jennings had done it."

"We'll never know."

They were quiet for a bit, listening to the radio. The station format seemed to be soft country and soon Beth was humming along to the Crystal Gayle song that came on.

"You sing like you know how to use your voice," he observed.

She looked surprised. "I never took formal voice lessons or anything, but I was in chorus in school and then in an *a cappella* group in college. That was actually pretty demanding."

"That would explain it."

"I guess. I've always regretted not learning an instrument, though. I took piano lessons when I was little, but since my parents had to fight with me to get me to practice, they eventually stopped them."

"What instrument would you play if you could?" he asked.

She frowned, thinking. "I guess probably the guitar since I'd be able to accompany myself singing and you can take it anywhere."

"I could teach you."

As soon as the offer was out of his mouth he could have kicked himself. He'd tried giving lessons years ago as a way of making extra money and he'd hated every second of it. He didn't have the patience it took by a long shot. Nor did he have time for lessons while on tour. But the thought of sitting close to Beth, maybe even wrapping his arms around her to show her how to place her hands...

"Thanks, but that's okay. We both have other things we need to be doing."

Disappointment warred with relief at this, but he let it go. They drove without talking much after that, and his mind wandered back over the show last night and forward to that night's. He'd played Santa Cruz last year with another band and it had gone well, but he was expecting – hoping – for even better this time around.

Before long he'd tuned out the music and was turning over phrases and chord changes for the song he was working on. Part of why he loved road trips was how his mind had time to work on music without pressure. Ideas drifted in and out and songs came together. It was easier if he wasn't the one driving, since then he could write his ideas in a notebook as they came, but this was fine, too.

It was more than fine, actually. Even without talking, having Beth next to him made his day. She was peering out the window like everything they passed interested her. When they left Santa Barbara she'd watched the Pacific Ocean as long as she could, as if they were leaving it behind for good.

The 101 didn't run anywhere near the coast except at Morrow Bay, but they were coming up on it and it was pretty much the perfect spot to stop. He pulled off the road into the parking lot and turned the car off.

Beth was staring wide-eyed at the surfers.

"Let's go take a look," he said, climbing out.

Together they walked out onto the beach and watched the waves roll in. Fall was the best time of year for surfing out here, so there was a pretty good crowd on a nice day like today.

"Oh my God, how can they do that?"

He laughed, the wind carrying most of the sound away. "I don't know. I tried it once with a buddy when I was touring a few years back and I nearly drowned. It was one of my more humbling experiences."

"I'll bet. That's one experience I think I'll forego."

"Well, you could start smaller. In retrospect I should have had a couple lessons before I went out there."

She smirked at him, as if that would have been obvious to him if he weren't so arrogant. The next instant she was taking off her sandals, a wide grin on her face, her eyes bright.

"I've never walked on west coast sand before." A pause. "Or on east coast sand, for that matter. It feels good."

She took off toward the water, her strong calves flexing as her feet dug into the sand. Taking off his shoes he followed after her. Hell, he'd probably follow Beth over a damn cliff.

They stood for a few minutes with their feet in the water, watching surfers catch waves and ride them in. Beth yelped a few times when people went under, turning to him each time like he could do something about it.

"We'd better get going," she said finally, turning back toward the car.

She twisted in her seat so she could see the ocean on their left as they drove away, but soon the highway turned eastward and they lost the view. She settled back in her seat and scrolled through her iPod and he went back to the song he'd been working on.

He was listening to the bridge in his head, trying to figure out why it wasn't quite right, when he noticed she was harmonizing with the Everly Brothers. He darted a look at her but made no other move, afraid she'd get self-conscious and stop.

She'd created her own part, a sweet counterpoint to the main melody, and as soft as she was singing, he heard her clear and true. Her fingers tapped her thigh and she looked so perfectly content, so lost in herself and the music, he couldn't help smiling.

He could have listened to her every second of every mile they drove. Without even meaning to he began imagining how she'd sound on stage. It wasn't the craziest idea he'd had, though she'd probably think so. He needed to get her somewhere where they could try harmonies on "Better Off." For a while now he'd been thinking the song needed something else, maybe a different kind of vocal arrangement, but nothing he'd tried with the guys made sense. Because he needed a woman.

He needed Beth.

He already knew how they sounded singing together, so it was really a matter of getting her to try. He was pretty sure she'd look at him like he was nuts and turn him down if he asked her outright, though. He'd have to be more subtle about it, ask her for help. Beth couldn't refuse that kind of request. She was too nice.

The more he thought about it, the more excited he got. By the time they got to Santa Cruz he was amped, his mind whirling with new ideas. Just the thought of them gave him new energy, and he was practically bouncing off the walls through soundcheck.

That night he worked the fans like an evangelizing preacher proving their faith was justified. As if converting them all to his message was necessary for his personal salvation. Which it more or less was. Every note he played seemed to pour straight into the mass of people dancing and wild-eyed at his feet. Kind of like he was fucking them all at once. Every so often the crowd parted and he caught a glimpse of Beth at the table toward the back of the club, dancing and sweaty, taken over by the music, and he didn't know which he wanted more, to play for her or sleep with her.

He slapped Will's back as they left the stage. "We were totally in the pocket, man. A freight train couldn't have thrown us off."

Will looked surprised but gave something close to a smile.

"Dude, we totally killed out there," Matt said, beaming and sweaty. "That was one of the best shows all tour. Did you feel it?"

"Hell, yeah, I felt it. There's nothing better, is there?"

"Not even sex," Brian chimed in.

Jesse started to laugh, but Brian was dead serious.

"It's true," Matt said. "Music is bigger than sex. Or like, sex is one way to get that big, mystical feeling you get with music. Except I get it all the time when we play, and hardly ever when I have sex."

Jesse gaped at Matt. He'd just put into words exactly what Jesse felt. Brian was nodding, as if he, too, shared the sentiment.

Then Matt grinned his shit-eating grin. "Lucky for us we get to play *and* get laid." He looked at Brian. "Ever think of taking advantage of all the girls, Brian? Your old woman would never know."

Brian just looked at him, his face devoid of expression. "No."

Jesse was only half-paying attention, though. He was too busy thinking about what Matt had said. He hadn't yet met a woman who could compete with how he felt when he was playing, on or off stage. That was part of the problem, and the reason he'd always found it so easy to go on tour even when he had girlfriends. It was also the reason he'd sworn off serious relationships.

All his girlfriends had fallen for him after they saw him play, but soon enough they resented the fact that music took up so much of his life. The first time a woman had demanded he spend more time with her and less playing music he'd been confused, but when it kept happening he felt betrayed. How could they like him and still want him to give less to it? No one who understood him would have asked it of him.

So he kept things casual these days, an easy enough thing to do, especially since girls he slept with on the road didn't expect more than a night. There was nothing mystical about it, but it scratched the itch.

Tonight he'd hopefully be going back to the hotel with Beth, but it would be for music, not sex. If it worked out like he hoped, it might not be such a bad trade-off.

He washed up in the bathroom and changed into a cleanish shirt. By the time he got to the green room a crowd had already formed. Beth came a while later after packing up the table, and while she looked happy enough to be there, she was obviously tired. Maybe she wouldn't mind leaving early and helping him out.

She smiled when he brought her a bottle of water. "Thanks," she said, taking a long swallow.

"Let me know when you're taking off. I'm catching a ride with you."

"Oh, okay." She looked like she wanted to ask what the deal was, but stopped herself.

She wasn't the only one holding back. He came close to asking her yet again if she'd enjoyed the show just to hear her tell him how much she loved it, but managed to check his ego in time. The image of her dancing to his music was going to have to be enough. That and the damp strands of hair that clung to her temples.

They wandered off in opposite directions and Jesse met up with friends he hadn't seen since he'd been through a year before. It was great seeing them, but when they announced the party was moving to their place, he declined to go.

"You go ahead," he said. "I'm sure the guys will want to go, but I have some stuff I have to work on."

"Sounds mysterious," his friend commented.

"Not really," he said. "I'm going into the studio a couple weeks after the tour ends and I need to finish some songs."

"All right, man. Far be it from me to get between you and your art. You know where we are if you change your mind."

A little while later people started filtering out. Jesse excused himself from the two girls who'd been hanging around him all night and found Beth. Soon they were driving through the dark streets.

"Stu said something about getting you a gig on one of the late shows," she said. "That'd be pretty amazing."

"Yeah. I've learned not to count chickens, though. Until the deal is signed I'm just assuming it won't happen."

"Huh. I don't think I could manage that."

"You would if you'd been disappointed enough," he said.

"I suppose you're right. I'd probably have a hard time believing in another guy."

He had nothing to say to that. It didn't have anything to do with him, but somehow it depressed him to hear her say it.

Beth pulled into the Howard Johnson's parking lot and turned off the car.

"Do you think you could come listen to something for a minute?" he asked. "I've been working on a song, and I was wondering if you could help me with it."

"How could I possibly help?"

"I want to try some harmonies."

"But I–"

"I won't keep you up late. Let's just give it a whirl and see how it goes."

She sat there biting her lip like the fate of the world depended on how she answered.

"This is strictly business," he said. "I won't even flirt. I swear."

He got out of the car and grabbed his bag and guitar, hoping he could build some momentum by moving.

Still she hung back, her doubt evident. But he was patient, or he could pretend to be. He stood there, waiting while she thought it all through. He already knew she'd come around. Beth wanted to try new things but she had to drive herself crazy before she did any of them.

"Okay, I'll do it. As long as it doesn't take more than an hour or so. I've got more promo kits to send out tomorrow morning, and some updates to your website."

"No problem."

Beth followed him up the stairs to the third floor and down the hallway to his room. It should have felt titillating, but it didn't. Or not much, anyway. He was in work mode, clear-headed and ready to make things happen.

Then he opened the door, flicked on the light and saw the bed. Hotel rooms were pretty much all about the bed. They were both going to have to pretend the bed had nothing to do with them. He didn't want Beth getting all skittish, not when he needed her help.

Luckily he hadn't had time to make a mess yet. Walking farther into the room he turned on every light, hoping to dispel any feeling of intimacy. He would have killed for a shower, but taking one with Beth in the room was not going to fly.

"Want some water?" he asked, determined to be a good host.

She was still standing in the doorway. Definite flight risk.

"Sure, that'd be great," she said, finally coming the rest of the way into the room.

The door slammed behind her and she jumped, then laughed self-consciously. Grabbing a plastic cup from the tray near the microwave, he went into the bathroom and filled two cups. When he came out he found her sitting on the desk chair on the other side of the room.

Taking his acoustic guitar out of its case he climbed onto the bed and leaned up against the headboard, boots and all.

"So here's the thing," he began, tuning the guitar as he spoke. "I've been working on a song, and I think it needs a female vocalist on harmonies. I want to hear you sing it and I'll know if I'm on the right track."

"But I don't know what I'm doing. I'm not a professional singer," she protested.

"You know how to use your voice, though. That's what's important. We're just playing around, seeing how it sounds. You can sing on key and you can harmonize. That's all I need."

She looked dubious, but she sat up straighter, a gleam in her eye like she was ready for business. "Okay then, fire away and I'll see what I can do."

"I'll play the song through first, and you just listen and think about how you might sing along. I'll play it through again and you can jump in. You can start with the chorus and see what happens after that."

She nodded and took a sip of water, her eyes on him.

***

The song sounded familiar, and at first she thought it was just that she was used to his rhythms and the sound of his voice, but after a few bars she recognized it as the tune he occasionally hummed under his breath when he was filling up on gas or stringing his guitar. She hadn't realized he was thinking about music constantly, even when he seemed to just be humming absently.

It was a love song, if you could call it that. He sang about being better off without his lover, and at some points in the song the chorus was bitter as he sang "I'm better off without you." At other points it was more tender and apologetic, "you'll be better off without me, too."

It was beautiful, though an edge crept in occasionally, sometimes in the fierce way he played, sometimes in they way he sang the lyrics. Before he was through she thought she understood what he was asking for and she was eager to sing along. If she'd heard it on the radio, she'd have been singing along with it, anyway.

She watched his hands as he played the last few bars, letting the song trail off into silence.

"What do you think?"

I think you're the sexiest man I've ever met.

She'd never say it, shouldn't even think it in case he somehow read it off of her. But she wasn't any different than all those fans who wanted him. He was insanely lust-worthy, even more so now than at his shows. He wasn't performing, and in fact she had the feeling she was seeing a truer part of him. Serious and intent, focused on his music, trying to be better.

"It's a great song," she said, even though that's not what he'd been asking. He wasn't looking for compliments, but she gave it anyway. "I think I get what you're looking for. Just let me know if I'm off track."

"We'll just go with whatever comes out. We don't have to get it the first time, or even tonight."

The thought of another night sitting like this in his hotel room started her heart pounding, so she pushed it out of her thoughts. This was work to him, nothing more. Not at the moment anyway.

So they tried it again with her singing along on the chorus, and it sounded good, she could tell it did. Then they did the whole song through and he was smiling when they finished.

"That was even better than I was hoping for. Let's try it again, but this time let's try it a bit darker and see what happens."

She relaxed after a few more tries, no longer worried that she wasn't giving him what he wanted. She dipped in and out when it felt right, sometimes echoing Jesse, sometimes right along with him.

"That was awesome," he said, leaning forward, his eyes shining in the light from the bedside table. "Your instincts are perfect. Maybe I'll do something a little different this time."

He spent a few minutes trying other things, his face intent, all his focus inward. Beth shifted in the chair trying to get comfortable before giving in and moving to the bed, where she sat cross-legged on the corner opposite from Jesse.

She smiled to herself, feeling silly for how she over-thought everything. Yes, she was sitting on his bed. No, he was not about to ravage her. In fact, once he started writing in his notebook he didn't seem to notice she was there at all.

Which meant she could admire the way his lean muscles moved every time he shifted, and the way his hair fell in front of his eyes as he frowned in concentration. She was as incapable of turning away from him now as she had been when he'd been on stage.

He looked up from his notes and caught her staring, but all he did was smile.

"I think I've got it," he said, and started playing.

Without having to say anything else they were in it, singing the song clear through without missing a beat. They were both grinning when they finished.

"We make a good team. Which was why I was thinking that you should sing it with me on stage one of these nights."

The idea was so ludicrous she just laughed.

"I'm serious. There'd be nothing to it and you'd be doing me a big favor."

"Jesse, that's insane. What makes you think I'd be any good? You know better than anyone performing isn't the same as singing in a car. Or a hotel room. Besides, the thought terrifies me."

"You performed with your *a cappella* group, didn't you?"

"That was different. There were a bunch of us on stage, and...it was just different. It was mostly friends and family coming to see us. It doesn't even compare to playing sold-out shows where people are screaming your name."

"You just need to do the same thing on stage that we did tonight. I want this to go on the next album and playing it live will help me work out the arrangements."

"That's...I can't..."

"Just think about it. We'll practice it some more and you'll get more confidence." He studied her. "It's a pretty big rush, you know."

"If you live through it."

He gave her a look and started to play again, only this time with lyrics that were clearly made up on the spot.

Come on, Beth, you know you want to
This is how we get our kicks
Come on, Beth, you know you want to
We'll be like Don Henley and Stevie Nicks

Reaching over she grabbed a pillow from the head of the bed and lobbed it at him.

"Really? That's what I get for offering you the chance of a lifetime?"

"Maybe I'm not ready for the chance of a lifetime."

She'd meant to be flippant but it didn't quite come out that way. It came out with the ring of truth, God help her. Jesse's smile faded and he studied her. He was strumming lightly now, probably not even conscious of what he was doing. She could make out each grain of late-night stubble, each individual eyelash as they veiled his eyes, and her entire body lit up with awareness.

They sat like that, just looking at each other for several long beats. Then someone knocked on the door. Both of them started, shaking the bed.

Jesse set his guitar aside. "What the...?"

Another knock, louder this time, and Jesse got off the bed and looked through the peephole. "What the hell..."

"Jesse? Are you in there?"

A woman's voice. Beth sat frozen in place as Jesse opened the door. A girl she recognized from the party stood there, her face lighting up at the sight of him. Then she noticed Beth and her face fell.

"Oh I..."

Beth stood up. "I was just going," she said, jamming her feet into her shoes.

The girl's face went from miserable to confused but hopeful, and for a second Beth felt for her.

Jesse stood there, looking pained. "Beth, wait..."

"I'll see you tomorrow," she said, forcing a smile as she passed by him and out the door.

Then she was home free and hurrying down the hallway as fast as she could without actually breaking into a run.

The crazy thing was she felt a lot like she had walking in on Jeff and yogurt girl, but that didn't make any sense. She and Jesse weren't seeing each other, which meant he couldn't cheat on her. Logically she knew her reaction was absurd, but it didn't help. She pictured Jesse letting that girl into his room, kissing her, taking off her clothes. And it hurt. There was no denying that.

But maybe this was for the best. Better she get her head on straight now rather than later. She couldn't afford to be a fool again.

Chapter Five

Jesse watched Beth disappear out the door and turned to Heidi.

"What are you doing here?"

He sounded harsher than he meant to and she blinked, her face flushing.

"I...I asked Will where you'd gotten to and he said you were here. He told me your room number and said you'd be happy to see me."

That little prick. It wasn't like Will to throw women his way, so he could only guess he was making sure nothing happened between him and Beth. He'd suspected Will had a thing for her, but this confirmed it.

Heidi stood there looking mortified and he realized he hadn't let her in yet. She was pretty and sweet and fun, and they'd had a good time last year when he came through. Spending the night with her would be easy and uncomplicated, just the way he liked it. He was horny from spending hours with Beth, pent-up from looking without touching.

But he just wasn't feeling it.

"I'm really sorry, Heidi. Now's not a good time."

He couldn't believe the words were even coming out of his mouth, but he didn't take them back.

She let out a breath. "I'm sorry I busted in on you and that woman. I didn't realize..."

"It wasn't your fault. Maybe next time, huh?"

"Sure, Jesse."

"You okay to get home?"

"Yeah, I'm good."

"You take care now."

She gave him a little smile and walked away. Two women chased away in five minutes. That had to be a record.

He paced around the room, full of restless energy as he imagined knocking Will around.

Except he couldn't.

Nothing was supposed to happen between him and Beth, nothing *had* been happening, so he had no right to pick a fight over the fact that Will had sent a hot girl to his door. Technically speaking, he should have been thrilled.

But apparently he'd rather hang out with Beth with no sex in sight than have mindless, no strings sex with some other girl.

He was totally fucked.

***

Beth was organizing her car the next day when Will came out. "Mind if I ride with you today? If I don't get a break from that van I'm gonna lose it."

"Oh, sure," she said, taken aback.

For some reason she'd fallen into thinking that only Jesse could ride with her, but just because Jesse thought that didn't make it true. Besides, she could use a little space right now. She was starting to feel possessive of him, and that was not okay, though it wasn't surprising given how her days revolved around him. This morning she'd had to sort through dozens of photos of him for his Facebook page, all the while trying not to feel anything.

Will smiled like she'd just made his day and grabbed his stuff. He was just tossing it in her car when Jesse came out, his bags and guitar in hand. He said nothing, just stopped and looked from Will to her.

"Will's riding with me today," she said, trying to sound casual, annoyed by the twinge of guilt she felt.

For a second Jesse looked like he was going to deck Will. Then his gaze fell on her and his expression softened into resignation.

"Sure, whatever. I'll see you in Portland."

"So, how're you liking things so far? Is it what you expected?" Will asked as she pulled out ahead of the van.

"I can't say I expected anything in particular, but I'm enjoying the music." Since Jesse's prowess seemed to be a sore spot she decided not to say any more on that topic. "I'm looking forward to seeing more of the country. That's my main goal."

"Well, you came at a good time. We spent the last few weeks in the Midwest, and I don't think I've ever been so bored."

"I can imagine. What do you plan to do when the tour ends? Do you have some other gig lined up, or do you work other kinds of jobs?"

"Well, that depends. Jesse hasn't said yet whether he wants me on the album he's recording after the tour. I'm leaving things open in case he does, but if not I'll try to scare up some other work when I get back to Austin. I've done some session work in LA too, so that's an option."

"I'm not sure I could handle so much uncertainty. I guess you must be used to it, though."

"I suppose, but it'd be nice if he gave me a hint. I don't know what he's waiting for. I wouldn't put it past him to leave me hanging for the fun of it."

Jesse struck her as far too straightforward to do that. It seemed more likely he either hadn't made up his mind or he didn't want to rock the boat while they were still on tour.

"Is that why you're so angry at him?" she asked, her curiosity getting the better of her.

Everyone seemed to like Jesse, so she couldn't help wondering why a guy who was obviously benefiting from him would be so bitter.

Will shifted in his seat, his mouth tightening. "I never said I was angry. I just get annoyed that things fall in his lap. I don't think he appreciates what he's got."

That didn't square with what she knew of Jesse, or what Stu had said for that matter. Jesse worked nearly every minute of the day on his music, in one way or another, and a man who'd lived in his car probably didn't take anything for granted. Will's attitude sounded more like straight-up jealousy, but she'd already heard more than she cared to.

Thoughts of Jesse led to last night and the woman at his door. No doubt he'd slept with her. Were women interchangeable to him? Did he even like her?

"I remember you from college," Will said.

She shook her head and made herself focus on the conversation at hand.

"What do you mean? I just met you."

"You worked at the coffee shop on campus. I used to stop in there once or twice a week."

"That's funny. I don't remember you. I'm usually good with faces, but then again I did see a lot of people when I worked there."

"Yeah, I had a beard then, too, so I looked different. I always thought you were cute, though."

She wasn't sure what to say, so she more or less ignored the compliment. "I hated that job, partly because everyone seemed to recognize me and I was so shy. I only worked there for a semester, then I got a job in the library."

She wasn't sure where to go from there. Conversation never felt this labored with Jesse, nor did his flirting make her inwardly wince. The silence that descended wasn't comfortable either, so she filled it by asking him about the bands he'd played in. She hadn't been much of a party-goer, so she never saw him play anywhere, a fact that seemed to further demoralize him.

By the time they got to Portland she was dying to get out of the car. Unfortunately Will announced he was hungry and suggested they stop for a bite to eat. They managed that without any conversation pitfalls, but there was still something off about it, like he was hoping for more from her.

Instead of feeling flattered she felt cornered and resentful. It wasn't his fault, not really, but she wasn't looking to repeat the ordeal tomorrow, or any other time. Better to nip it in the bud now.

***

They'd been in the van for about twenty minutes when Stu glanced into the back seat. Both Brian and Matt had their headphones on and were listening to their own music, eyes closed and heads lolling against the seats.

"So what's the deal? Have you slept with her?"

"What are you talking about?" Jesse asked, instinctively defensive.

"Don't play dumb with me, Jesse," Stu said.

Jesse sighed. "No, I haven't slept with her."

"But there's something going on, right? I know I'm not imagining things."

"I like her, okay? I actually like her, and yeah, I'd love to have sex with her, but I get that it's a bad idea. She wouldn't go for it anyway. You told her not to and for some reason she cares about that. Plus I get the feeling she's not too impressed by my lifestyle." He blew out a breath. "There's just this tension between us, even when I'm not trying for anything."

"Great. So what you're saying is there's mutual attraction and it's growing stronger as you both deny yourselves."

Jesse said nothing.

"I never should have hired her. The last thing I need is to have this whole thing blow up in my face."

"Beth's doing a great job, better than anyone else would, and you know it," Jesse said, his fists clenching in his lap. "She's doing all kinds of things we should have been doing before –"

"No shit, Jesse. Which is why you need to keep your pants zipped around her. You can have any other woman you want. How many guys can say that?"

Jesse grunted and turned his head to look out the window. He knew enough not to tell Stu that he didn't give a shit about all the other women he could be sleeping with. Stu was right. He needed to cool things down before they got any hotter. No more late nights in his hotel room. That was pushing it. And maybe he needed to stop being so possessive and let the other guys drive with her.

But he wasn't going to give up on the song they'd worked out together. That was different.

***

The drive with Will left Beth with a tension headache, but luckily the hotel, as rundown as it was, had a halfway decent pool. There was nothing like cutting through the water with long sure strokes to wash away irritation. She did her usual forty lengths and climbed out, her muscles pleasantly fatigued.

She grabbed a towel and had just begun drying off when Jesse walked through the glass door. Quickly she wrapped the towel around her middle and tucked it between her breasts. At least she wasn't standing in front of him in nothing but a tank suit, and she was more or less as covered, but she still felt oddly vulnerable. At least he couldn't see what her nipples were doing.

Or could he? The way he was looking at her, she felt like he was seeing all sorts of things.

"My room's down the hall," he said, by way of explanation. "Good swim?"

"Yes, thanks. Clears out the cobwebs."

"I've never been much of a swimmer, but I've never turned down a hot tub."

She glanced over at the hot tub on the other side of the pool. "Public ones kind of oog me out."

"And pools don't?"

"Only if I think about it, which I try not to do."

"Funny. That's how I cope with most things."

Was he trying to tell her something, or just making idle conversation?

She was shivering now. Abandoning her towel she picked her swim wrap off a lounge chair and pulled it on. Now she was marginally more modest, though the blue terry cloth clung to her breasts and thighs. She slid her feet into flip flops.

"I need to shower, then I'll meet you in the lobby and we can head to the radio station."

He nodded and turned to go, then seemed to change his mind. "Will sent Heidi to me last night. Gave her my room number and everything."

"Oh. That was...nice of him."

"No, it wasn't. You may have noticed the guy doesn't go out of his way to do me favors. He must have seen us leave together and worried something would happen."

That certainly squared with what she knew of Will, especially after the drive today.

"That's pretty low," she said, at a loss. "I'd say I can't believe it, but I suppose I can."

"Yeah, well, I just wanted you to know that. Also, I didn't sleep with her."

She kept her expression from betraying the relief that washed over her. "It wouldn't have been my business if you had."

"Maybe not, but the whole thing was pretty tacky."

"I won't argue with that," she said. "Are tours always this petty and prone to drama?"

"You haven't seen anything, honey," he said, his smile breaking through at last, the effect hot enough to dry every last drop of water on her. "We might as well be in high school."

"In that case, I'll save you a spot on the bus tomorrow."

He was still smiling as he pushed through the door and out into the hallway, disappearing from view.

***

The next day Jesse was leaning against her car, arms crossed, his chin on his chest. His hair hid his face, but he was either sleeping or trying to. She hit the unlock button on her key and the car beeped, making him jump upright. It took him a second to focus, but when he did he gave her a lazy smile more suited to a bedroom than a parking lot at noon.

She felt herself flush and only hoped he was too out of it to notice. "Hey, there. Have you been waiting long?"

"Naw, just a couple minutes. But I can sleep anywhere." He grabbed a paper cup from the roof of her car. "Brought you a coffee."

"Oh, wow. Thanks. That's so nice of you."

She took a tentative sip and found it was just the way she liked it, one sugar and a little cream. She smiled her pleasure and took another sip.

"Don't think I haven't been paying attention," he said, giving her a raised eyebrow. He stashed his guitar and bags in the car. "Why don't you let me drive today. You enjoy the…"

He trailed off, his eyes getting hard, and she didn't have to turn around to know Will had come out.

"Hey, Will," she said, trying to sound casual.

His eyes darted between her and Jesse. "You left early last night. Where'd you go?"

Clearly he was trying to get a handle on whether anything had happened between them.

"I was just tired and I had a lot to do this morning," she said.

Jesse remained silent, giving away nothing.

Will's shoulders eased out of their hunch, like maybe he'd decided to believe there was nothing to worry about. "Right. Well, I guess I'll talk to you later. If Jesse doesn't need you, that is," he said, sparing a dark glance Jesse's way before heading to the van a few spots over.

Jesse glared after him. "If he bothers you, you tell me and I'll take care of it."

"I'm sure that won't be necessary."

"Beth."

"Okay, yes, I'll tell you."

Stu came out a minute later and she conferred with him a few minutes. Finally she and Jesse were on their way, everyone else's issues and idiosyncrasies falling away behind them.

Not that she was rid of Will altogether. As expected he came up to her that night at the after party.

"You know, if Jesse bothers you, you can tell Stu. You don't have to do everything he says. I mean, just because he wants to ride with you every day doesn't mean you can't say no."

"It's fine, Will," she said, trying to contain her exasperation. "Jesse's not forcing me to do anything."

She wasn't sure if he believed her, though. He seemed bent on thinking she only spent time with Jesse because she had to, and she didn't feel like spelling it out for him. Luckily there wasn't much time for him to bother her, since she was either running around before the show, in the middle of a crowd of people, or in the car with his arch nemesis.

Jesse caught a cold after Olympia and his voice started to go, which meant no singing with him in the car. He spoke as little as possible, too, which was too bad. She'd gotten used to hearing his stories, but just sitting next to him was more fun than anything else she could think of.

She bought a box of Throat Coat tea and made him drink it before his performances in Seattle and Spokane, ignoring his scowls since she was pretty sure he secretly liked being fussed over. He even seemed to heed her advice and drank less alcohol and more water. He was too run-down to show her around Seattle, but she spent a few hours before the show walking around Pike's Place.

It wasn't until they were on their way to Missoula that he reached back over the seats and pulled out his guitar. He had to hold it at a weird angle so that the head stock was sticking up near her shoulder, but somehow he managed. He spent a few minutes tuning it before pulling a pick out of his pocket and starting the song they'd practiced together.

She was so flustered she didn't even sing.

"What's the matter?"

"Nothing. I just thought we were done with that."

"Why would you think that?"

This was clearly a rhetorical question, since Jesse immediately began singing. She came in like she was supposed to, because after all this was easy and fun and her heart grew light as their voices blended together. They were both smiling when they'd finished.

"We'll try this out at soundcheck tonight," he said, like it was a done deal. "If all the kinks are worked out I'll put it on the set list."

Her hands tightened on the steering wheel. "Are you crazy? I can't sing with you. I'll be terrified."

"Well, sure. But terror's only part of it. The other part is the crazy high you get."

"Maybe you get high. I'll probably faint."

"I went to a record store before we left today and I found some great vinyl, including that Waylon Jennings album, 'Leather and Lace.' I've been looking for it for ages, and today I finally found it."

"That's great."

"It's also a sign."

"A sign of what?"

"That you should sing with us."

"You're laying it on kind of thick, aren't you?"

"Come on, honey. It'll be fun and it'd mean a lot to me. And if you hate it, that'll be that. I won't bother you anymore."

She didn't say anything right away, but she was a goner and she knew it. Was there any woman who could resist that plea? He probably called every female he met "honey," but when he said it to her, her whole body answered *yes*.

"Okay, I'll sing at soundcheck. But I'm not promising anything," she said, her voice stern, as if that would prove she wasn't a pushover.

He beamed at her. "I knew you'd do it."

Her heart thudded hard once, then twice. She pushed his guitar away. "Careful with that thing. You keep poking me with it."

"Aw, that's what all the girls say."

***

Usually she helped move the gear into a club, took a few pictures, set up the table, and caught up on band email or social media updates. Sometimes she made a run to a liquor store. But not today. Today she'd been dumb enough to agree to sing.

They'd just set up and were going through the usual routine when Jesse told the band he wanted to run through all of "Better Off."

Will scowled at him. "Seriously? We've never even played that outside of rehearsal."

"No kidding. But I've tinkered with it and think it's ready now. Is that a problem?" Jesse asked, his eyes hard.

Everyone in the band tensed, watching the two men. Beth's heart started hammering away in her chest and for some reason she felt guilty, like it was her fault. But whether it was or not, she was at least part of the reason for the tension between Will and Jesse.

Finally Will looked away. "Whatever," he muttered. "Let's just get on with it."

Wait until he found out she'd be singing with them. She closed her eyes and did breathing exercises, in and out slowly, letting her lungs expand. She was just singing, that was all. She hadn't promised anything except to give it a try. She could still back out.

"You ready, Beth?" Jesse called.

Will's head snapped up. "What does she have to do with it?"

"We're gonna try it with her singing harmony," Jesse replied, his answer clipped, a clear signal it wasn't up for discussion.

"Huh? Since when does Beth sing?" Matt asked, looking bewildered.

"We've been practicing, and she's a great singer," Jesse said.

Beth wished for the stage to open up and swallow her.

Will wasn't backing down. "You could have said something."

"I just fucking did. Can we get on with it?" he asked, glaring around at everyone.

Brian shrugged. "Sure, man. Let's do it."

Jesse turned back to Beth, his glare turning to an encouraging smile. She looked at Will, who was glaring back at her, then at Brian and Matt. They seemed more curious than anything. Stu was frowning off to the side, but he didn't say a word. This was Jesse's show.

Beth set down her phone, which she'd been using to take pictures, and walked up the steps to the stage, stopping when she was next to Jesse. Her entire body was shaking, her stomach clenching as she looked out to where several hundred people would be watching tonight. People who paid to see Jesse, not some temporary assistant road manager who didn't know what she was doing.

Jesse set a microphone in front of her and adjusted it to the right height. "Relax, honey. We're just singing like we did in the car, all right?"

She released a breath, nodding her understanding. Brian counted off and the band kicked in. Then Jesse started to sing, and suddenly she was enveloped in the whole sound, surrounded and flooded by the music.

It threw her off a bit, having only heard the song with Jesse's guitar, but once she focused in on him she knew where she was supposed to be. She came in on cue, though her voice shook and sounded kind of reedy. It also took her a minute to get the hang of how to sing into the mic, so they were halfway through the song before she found her footing.

Jesse sang right to her so that it was like a conversation between lovers and they were playing off each other. The sound of the whole band playing together carried her along, lifting her up and setting her back down.

Jesse's guitar was the last instrument playing, and then that too faded into silence.

"Holy shit," Brian said.

"I know, right?" Jesse said, beaming all around, then at her. He pulled her close in a one-armed hug and planted a smacking kiss on her cheek. "Don't even try to tell me you can't do this."

The guys were all talking now, sounding excited, though when Beth glanced over, Will still looked sullen. There wasn't time to worry about it, though, because Jesse wanted to run through it again. Everything came together again even easier than before. She looked only at Jesse, letting him lead her into the song, watching him for cues, and they blended perfectly, as tight as they'd been singing together in her car.

Then it was over, and she stood in the silence between the song and whatever came after that, as dazed as if she'd woken up from a long dream. Then someone clapped, the sound a jolt back into reality.

The club's manager came forward, a huge grin splitting his face. "That was awesome. You're gonna kill tonight. I only wish I'd been able to get you guys for two nights."

"Thanks, man," Jesse said. "It's good to be back."

Stu stood in front of the stage, arms crossed at his chest, his expression unreadable. He didn't look the least bit pleased with that he'd heard. What if he was angry she'd blurred the lines of her position?

She should have mentioned this to him before, but she'd assumed Jesse would take care of it.

Jesse looked over at him. "What do you think? It's good right?"

"It works. When will you play it?"

Before Jesse could reply Beth jumped in. "Can I get it over with early on?" she asked, her voice breaking like some nervous prepubescent boy. So much for her great pipes. "If I have to wait too long I might lose it."

"Sure. We'll do it early on in the first set. Maybe fourth or fifth. I'll work on the set list."

"Fine, then," Stu said. "Let's finish up here so we can eat."

Beth left the stage to the band and grabbed her phone, uploading the new photos. Like always she took care of all the little things that needed doing, but in the background her mind continually spun, trying to compute what would happen tonight. She couldn't imagine it, couldn't even visualize herself making that long walk to the stage.

When she was a kid and she used to try to picture certain things happening, maybe a fun trip that was coming up, or her part in a school play. They were usually things that she looked forward to and feared in equal measure. Oftentimes her poor over-taxed brain couldn't conjure images of what the event would be like, probably because as a kid she had no context for some of the new experiences she was going through. But some weird, dark part of her decided it was because she'd be dead by then.

She never told that to anyone, aware of how morbid and bizarre it was. She'd both believed it and also knew it to be ludicrous, especially as she did survive and lived through all the events, and they were never as scary or exotic as she imagined they'd be.

But tonight the idea that she'd be getting up on stage in front of hundreds of people and singing was so out of the range of possibility her brain went dark at the thought. So maybe this time she really would bite it before the big moment, in which case she had nothing to worry about.

She forced herself to eat a few bites of fried chicken she'd brought back for everyone. The guys talked around her and she tried to participate in order to not think about what was ahead, but as usual they were talking about stuff she didn't know a thing about. Opening acts, other gigs they'd played, dumb things they'd done while drunk.

Jesse caught her eye a couple times and smiled, as if to reassure her, but all she could manage was a tight smile back. By the time they were done eating she was wound so tight, you could have bounced a quarter on her.

She was mulling over the various ways she could screw up when Jesse came over with a beer.

"Here, have this. It'll take the edge off."

"No, thanks. I need to stay sharp. I don't want to screw up."

"Honey, there's a good reason musicians drink, and the state of your nerves is one of them. A couple beers won't kill you."

She stared at the beer, unsure.

"There are decades of empirical research behind me on this."

She huffed out a laugh and grabbed the bottle. "Fine, you win. Got any valium while we're at it?"

"You're gonna be great, Beth," he said, suddenly serious. "I wouldn't have you get up on stage if I wasn't dead sure of that."

She hadn't thought of it that way. Of course he didn't want a train wreck during his show, so he must really believe in her. On the other hand, his faith seemed misguided, and yet another reason for her to freak out. Screwing up would not only wreck the show, it would let him down.

"I don't know why you're so sure of that."

"Hey, I'm the expert here, right? So trust me. You're ready. If this shit was rocket science, none of us would be up there."

She made a face at him, but he'd made her feel better. She took a long pull of her beer and let out a sigh. "You don't have to babysit me. I'll be fine, especially now that I have orders to drink."

"My work here is done," he said, squeezing her arm once before heading backstage.

She listened to the opening act, a cute young guy named Max, do his soundcheck, all the while working on her second beer and responding to tweets on behalf of the band. The social media thing was kind of a never-ending job but she liked feeling that she was helping fans connect.

She was just finishing her beer and debating a third when Jesse came over.

"Feel like taking a walk?" he asked.

She was feeling slightly calmer now, the panic diluted by alcohol.

"Sure, it's a nice night," she agreed.

"We'll be back in a bit," Jesse called to the room in general, leading her out of the main room, down a hallway and out a back door until they stood in the dusky light of early evening.

The club they were playing tonight was smallish compared to the other places they'd been so far, but they were just a few blocks west of the university and Stu predicted the house would be packed. If she hadn't been about to perform she should have been pleased to hear it, but as it was she would have been happier if no one showed.

Missoula wasn't what she'd expected. It was pretty boring, actually, flat and laid out in a grid, though the mountains circled the town like wagons around a campfire, protective and comforting in the distance. A few blocks north of the club they came to a river that split the town in two. Along the banks the trees displayed their fall foliage splendor, glowing burnt umber and buttery gold.

"Wow, this is gorgeous," she breathed. "I had no idea we were so close to something this pretty."

Crossing a bike path they sat on a bench and watched the river flow by. Beth shivered as the wind picked up.

"Cold?" he asked, wrapping an arm around her.

Her body tensed up before gradually relaxing into his solid warmth. This was the closest she'd been to him, and though it was entirely non-sexual, she was aware of exactly where her body met his.

"I can't believe this is happening," she said, her breath misting in the air before them. "I didn't think anyone would go for me actually performing live."

"But they did, because it sounded amazing. You heard that, right? Didn't it feel good to be a part of it?"

She nodded, unable to meet his eye. It had felt good, almost too good to sing with Jesse, to feel part of it all. It scared her, because nothing that good could last. Either she'd ruin it or someone else would.

"You don't have to do it if you don't want to. You know that, right? I realize I pushed this on you pretty fast. Sometimes I get things in my head and I ignore anything that might slow me down."

"You're really not worried I'll screw up and ruin your show?" she asked.

"Everybody messes up, you just can't make a big thing of it. Even if you did cock it up, I'd say something charming and funny and everyone would love you even more."

She couldn't help smiling at that. It was true. He could do that.

She looked up at the "M" branded into the mountaintop in the distance, vaguely wondering what it meant and how it had gotten there. Maybe she'd ask someone, but probably she'd let it remain a mystery.

The last rays of the sun were warm on her face as she thought over what he'd just said. He'd given her an easy way out, but she didn't want it anymore. She wasn't doing this just because she couldn't say no to Jesse. Mixed in with all the abject fear was a buzz of excitement. The part of her that wasn't terrified was thrilled. It had felt great up there with the band, singing Jesse's beautiful song.

And hadn't she taken this job to experience new things, have some kind of adventure? This was better than anything she'd dreamed up.

"I don't have anything to wear."

"Sure you do. A pair of jeans and something on top is all you need. You can decide how much you want to flaunt your assets."

"Oh my God, I can't believe this is happening."

"You bet your ass it is, honey," he laughed.

By the time they got back to the club, it was nearly eight and the doors were going to open soon. Which meant it was time to get ready. She would have killed for a shower, but there hadn't been time. Also, they were crashing with some friends of Jesse's that night, so she suspected her chances of taking a shower were not good until at least tomorrow.

Instead she went into the bathroom with her toiletry kit, make-up and clothes and tried to make herself look like someone who should be on stage. Unfortunately, when she was done she still looked exactly like herself, so she put on more of everything because really, subtlety had no place tonight. She changed into her tightest jeans and a black tank top. She added dangly silver earrings and took stock of herself again, and now she looked kind of rock 'n roll. Or at least kind of alt-country, though her short black boots were all wrong. If tonight wasn't a disaster and Jesse still wanted her onstage again, she'd do a little shopping. Hell, maybe she'd do some shopping even if he didn't.

When she emerged from the bathroom she found everyone in the back room nursing drinks and noodling around on their instruments. They all looked up when she entered and Jesse whistled. Brian and Matt gave little catcalls. She laughed, relieved by the blatant validation of her efforts.

"Want another beer?" Jesse asked.

"I'd better not. Just keep playing, it relaxes me."

Matt started to play a Johnny Cash song and they all joined in, and before long Beth was almost not even thinking about being up on stage.

Almost.

People came in and out of the room, and every time the door swung open she heard the swell of noise from the crowd and the piped-in music. Finally the manager who'd clapped for them earlier came in.

"You're up, Max."

The musician grabbed his guitars and headed out to a chorus of "knock 'em dead" and advice not to be too good or he'd make the rest of them look bad.

Beth stood up to head out to the table. "So I'll just wait for you to call me up, I guess?" she asked Jesse.

"We're going to play 'In Your Dreams' third, and then 'Better Off,'" Jesse, said, glancing at the set list. "If you want you can come backstage then and wait, but I think it would be cool if you just came through the crowd and got onstage. Kind of like a surprise guest from the audience coming up."

"Okay, I'll do that. If I haven't expired from nervousness before then."

"You won't, you're tougher than that. And anyway, Missoula's always been an easy crowd. You've got nothing to worry about."

She couldn't help the snort that came out of her at that.

"What, I'm serious," Jesse said.

"I think this is one of those things you just have to do in order to know you can do it."

"That's exactly right. But that usually doesn't make people feel better, which is why I didn't say it."

"Right. Well, I'll see you on the other side," she said, then walked away like she wasn't in an agony of nerves.

Chapter Six

Her anxiety gathered steam even as people came to the table and browsed. She advised on shirt sizes and explained the chronological order of the CDs, all the while wondering what they would think when they heard her. It seemed like a nice crowd, at least. Every club had its own vibe, and this one was distinctly relaxed and friendly. There was lots of laughter from people gathered around the tables and an excited hum in the air. It helped that Jesse had been coming there for the past few years and he'd built up a strong following.

As soon as the band went on she began to wish she'd lobbied to sing at the very end. Preferably after everyone left.

Her heart thudded louder than Brian's drums when they started "In Your Dreams." What if she actually, literally threw up in front of the entire audience? Even Jesse couldn't charm away a pile of vomit.

She was shivering with nerves, her fingers numb, when the song ended.

"We've got a brand new song to sing for ya'all tonight, so new no one but the band has heard it, but we're gonna play it for you folks right now."

The crowd hooted and whistled. Little did they know.

Jesse smiled and strummed his guitar, in no rush at all. He knew how to work a crowd. Stu came over to man the table while she was on stage. Her face must have betrayed her terror, because Stu leaned down and spoke into her ear.

"You're gonna be fine."

"And if that wasn't exciting enough," Jesse was saying, "our good friend Beth Levine is going to come up here to sing it with me. Come on up here, honey."

He was smiling at her like they had a secret, but she couldn't move. Stu put a hand on her back, propelling her forward, and there wasn't any refusing it, no running away or giving into fear. Her breath was shallow, the club taking on the aspect of a dreamscape as she made her feet move.

The crowd had turned to see who Jesse was talking about, and they parted now to let her through. As she walked she saw their curious faces, felt the heat of all of them pressing against her. They were smiling and clapping, full of excited expectation.

After the first few feet she kept her eyes fixed on Jesse and let him reel her in, his eyes never leaving her, his smile sweet and devilish all at the same time. Then he was at the edge of the stage, taking her hand and leading her to the mic.

Everyone's eyes were on her and she froze at the immensity of it.

"Smile, sweetheart," Jesse whispered in her ear. "It's all good."

Beth smiled, a forced, artificial thing that took over her face, and then became real as she looked into the faces of the front row. They were all beaming, beside themselves with joy just to be there. She knew what they felt, because she felt it every night when she watched them play. She'd seen them every night for over a week and she hadn't tired of it yet.

Jesse started to play, a few solitary notes that were soon joined by the rest of the band. Beth moved closer to the microphone and grabbed on with both hands, grateful for something to hold onto, and listened for Jesse. She was so anxious to come in at the right time that she missed her cue, but the band circled back around and picked her up the second time around.

Then the music took over. The fear was gone after the first few bars and it was just her voice melding into something bigger, giving the song its high notes, her smoother vocals a counterpoint to Jesse's raw, scraped-out delivery.

Despite their personal differences, after so many weeks of touring the band was tight and in sync, loose without being sloppy. All their differences and personality quirks dropped away and it was just the music.

Caught between the band's power and the crowd's surging, ecstatic energy, she felt herself lift off, a vessel through which the music moved.

She looked at Jesse. His eyes were closed, his throat at the open neck of his shirt damp with sweat. Then he opened his eyes and turned to her, everything he was singing visible in their dark depths. They sang the last chorus looking at each other, echoing the same words, her higher voice twining with his.

The crowd was screaming even before the last notes faded away, quieting only when Jesse announced her name again.

He leaned over, his mouth at her ear, his breath fanning her heated skin. "You did it, baby."

She left the stage on shaking legs to weave through the crowd, dazzled by the beaming faces that turned toward her as she made her way back to the table.

"You did good," Stu said, his look considering, before turning his attention back to the band.

She shook with reaction, adrenaline still coursing through her veins with nowhere to go. Gradually her heartbeat slowed and she was able to breathe normally, but for the rest of the show she had to bite back the grin that threatened to take over her face.

She'd done it. And now she understood why other people wanted to do it so badly. It felt fantastic.

She watched the rest of the set and sold more stuff during the intermission, only this time she had people telling her how awesome she'd sounded.

"Are you part of the band?" a twenty-something girl asked, her expression conveying awe and envy.

"No," Beth laughed. "That was kind of an anomaly. I can sing and I'm already with the tour, so it kind of just worked out."

"I'd give anything to be there with him."

It struck her then how lucky she was. Yes, it was the most terrifying thing she'd ever done, but it was also the most amazing.

She got a bunch of compliments and questions from other people buying music and t-shirts. Many of them wondered why someone who'd just been on stage was standing behind the table, and she tried to explain while also making correct change and keeping the line moving.

She danced and shouted and clapped though the second set, adrenaline feeding her euphoria until she was in a near transcendent state.

The crowd's roar began as the band played the final notes of the last encore.

"See you next year, Missoula!" Jesse called, and there was more yelling and stomping and calls more for.

The band headed off stage and the houselights went up, a signal that even the most hopeful fans understood. People started to make their slow way out, but plenty of people stopped first at her table. She deflected as many comments and questions about her performance as she could, thanking people when they gave her compliments and directing them to the mailing list sheet.

The women actually freaked her out more than the men did. It was they who got too close to her, like they could get to Jesse if they touched her. They asked her questions about him, and about what she'd done to be there. Some of them might have been a little nutty, but most of them were probably normal women swept up in the glory that was Jesse, and that was something she understood.

Half an hour later everyone had finally cleared out. Stu had long since left to help load the gear back in the van, so Beth packed up the remaining items. By the time she'd pushed the last box of merchandise into her car and slammed the hatch her limbs were heavy with fatigue but adrenaline from the night's show still pumped through her.

She made her way back into the club, stopping at the storage room the band was using to drop off the duffel bag Jesse had left in the car. The door was halfway open so she pushed it open all the way and stepped inside.

"Oh, sorry. I didn't…"

Jesse was standing in the dressing room in his jeans and cowboy boots, the baby blue western style shirt he'd worn on stage hanging open. She tried not to stare at his bare skin, at the hair on his chest and arrowing down into his jeans.

He was lean and muscular, not a spare ounce on him. No wonder, the way he poured so much energy out on stage night after night.

"There you are," he said, a goofy smile blooming on his face like she was all he needed in the world.

Before she knew what hit her he'd laid a smacking kiss on her lips, wrapped his arms around her waist, and swung her around in a circle while making loud whooping noises.

She was laughing and dizzy by the time he set her down. "So you thought it sounded okay?"

"Are you kidding me? That was one hell of a debut."

"It was pretty fantastic," she admitted, smiling up at him.

They were standing so close she could see every whisker in his jaw, the lines of sweat from his temples. For several long, voluptuous moments they stared at one another, their excitement building and turning into a different kind of heat.

"I was just bringing you this," she said, picking up the bag she'd dropped, as if that would save her.

He took it from her and tossed it to the side. "Didn't you feel it out there? That was magic."

He was definitely a little drunk. Not falling down drunk, but loose and happy.

She took a step back. "I'd better get back to the… the uh…"

"What's your hurry?"

"Nothing. I just have things to do."

"Liar." A slow, devastating smile, like he knew all her secrets. "All you have to do now is celebrate."

He came toward her.

She took another step back. "What are you doing? I'm an employee."

"You're way more than that, honey."

"Jesse."

"I love it when you say my name," he murmured, his drawl like honey melting in the sun. "All husky and breathless."

He came toward her again, but this time she didn't move away. Reaching out, he hitched a finger through the belt loop of her jeans and tugged. She wasn't sure if she moved toward him or he came closer to her, but they were only inches apart, his breath soft in her hair.

"Damn, you smell good," he whispered.

She was too aware of him, aware of herself reacting to him, all throbbing pulse points and body heat.

"I'm all sweaty."

He ducked his head into the curve of her neck and breathed. "I know. I wish I'd done it to you."

"You did do it to me."

For a second he was utterly still, then he moaned low in his throat and pulled on her jeans until she fell against him. Before she had time to think his mouth was on hers in a deep, sloppy kiss that was somehow patient and urgent at the same time. As if he were mining every taste from her mouth but could do it all day.

Her resistance fell almost instantly.

Her hands parted his shirt and slipped inside, skimming over the golden brown skin. He said her name like a plea and dove deeper.

Here was the boy who ignored a snake bite to kiss his girl. She opened up to him, the rough scrape of his jaw sending flares of heat through her veins. His other hand cupped the back of her head, supporting her as he licked into her, tasting of beer and chocolate and the tang of sweat.

He was all around her, his heat, his scent, need rising off him and twining with hers. More. Now. She didn't even think the words. Her body demanded it, her hands slid over him, telegraphing it.

In some distant chamber in her brain she knew there was a reason to stop, but her need was so sharp and unrelenting she ignored it and tugged his hips closer. In answer he scooped her up by her ass and set her on the table, then stepped into the open vee of her legs. He was huge and hard against her, the position intimate and almost unbearably arousing.

Which was probably why she didn't notice the door opening wider, or anything else until Will stood there, his face blank with shock. Jesse hadn't seem him yet, he was too busy kissing his way down her throat, but he glanced up when she gasped and went still. One look at her face and he pulled away and turned around.

"I knew it," Will spat, looking from her to Jesse.

Jesse moved in front of her, as if to block her from Will's gaze. A gesture she appreciated since Jesse had rucked her shirt up to just beneath her bra and, unbeknownst to her, unbuttoned her jeans. She sorted herself out as Jesse confronted Will.

"Back off. This has nothing to do with you," Jesse ground out, the honey-laced drawl replaced with the hard rasp of his most bitter songs.

His back was to her, but she felt the fury radiate from him as he stared at his guitar player. Will was equally furious, maybe even more so. He looked as if he'd been betrayed.

"I knew her before you did. If it wasn't for me, she wouldn't even be here."

Her clothes back in place, she stood up and moved to Jesse's side. "Will, just leave it alone, okay?"

He turned on her. "I thought...I thought we..."

He gave her a last, bleak look and left, banging the door wide open on his way out.

Footsteps approached down the hallway and Jesse toed the door shut with his boot. It closed with a gentle snap and once again they were secluded together in quarters way too close for comfort. Even standing several feet apart the heat Will had doused came flooding back.

"Well, that was creepy," she said.

"You're quite the man-eater, aren't you?"

"Right, that's me." She pushed her fingers through her hair, hoping it looked halfway normal. "Do you think he'll tell anyone?"

"I wouldn't put it past him, but we'll just have to deal with it. Stu'll be pissed, but I can handle him."

"We need to forget this ever happened."

His eyes held hers. "I'm going to remember every sweet second of it. So will you," he added, and shucked his shirt.

Her mouth went dry at the sight of him bare from the waist up, the coiling snakes looking dangerous against all that golden skin. Her gaze dropped further and she sucked in a breath at the sight of him still huge and hard. Her nipples tightened into points that pushed against the thin tank top.

Of course she wouldn't forget. Why would she want to forget the single hottest event of her life? But that wasn't the point. The point was how to get through the rest of the tour.

She could feel herself flush and knew he saw exactly what was happening to her. But they'd already let things go too far.

"You know what I mean," she said.

"You mean pretend to forget." He sighed and pulled a clean shirt out of the duffel bag. "Go on now, honey. I need a minute."

She needed more than a minute, and she was dangerously close to going back for more, so she left, the image of him standing there in nothing but jeans and his cowboy boots burned into her brain.

Pretend to forget.

The party was in full swing backstage among the lights and cables, a bunch of musicians jamming to one side. She welcomed the noise and the chance to get lost in it. Besides, she was still pretty amped, and she understood now why musicians partied so much after a show. It took a while for the adrenaline rush to subside, and she'd only sung one song.

Jesse came in a few minutes after she did, and she spent the rest of the night aware of him in every nerve ending. She knew where he was at any given moment, who he was talking to, whether he was laughing or listening intently. When the party moved to a house a few blocks away she went with it, determined to have a good time. Fortunately she got caught up in a conversation with the opening band's manager. He was high on something and his hands shook, but he was a fount of information.

"Everyone's talking about Jesse," Ron told her. "This new album is doing things for him. You'll see, by the next tour he'll have a whole entourage. The guy'll never have to tune his own guitar again. They'll have their own guitar and drum tech, a sound guy, who knows what else. If you think these chicks are hot, wait until…" He realized who he was talking to and gave an apologetic smile. "Sorry, babe. Anyway, you get what I'm saying. Things'll be a lot more comfortable next time around, and ten times as crazy."

Beth scanned the kitchen and living room from the corner she was wedged into, noting the bongs, keg, gallons of hard liquor and several topless women. And that was just this floor. All the hardcore stuff was happening in the basement.

She gave Ron a raised eyebrow. "This isn't crazy?"

"What, this? This is nothing," he said, gesturing at the room with his cigarette. "Kid stuff."

"Luckily, I won't be here next–"

She was cut off mid-sentence by a crash. Turning around, she saw Jesse standing over a broken glass and spilled beer. She nearly laughed at the bewildered expression on his face, like a little kid whose ice cream had toppled off his cone.

A blond in skin-tight jeans and leopard-print top appeared at his side and grabbed his arm. Beth couldn't hear what she said, but the intent was clear. She was going to make it all better. Jesse looked up and smiled and the woman stuck her tongue down his throat. He was so drunk she nearly knocked him over, but he caught himself and laughed, his arms coming out to grab her shoulders.

That was all Beth saw before she turned away. But she felt them behind her while she tried to focus on what Ron was saying, and after a few minutes she'd had enough. She'd played her part, but that didn't mean sticking around to watch Jesse get it on with another woman.

The band was crashing that night at the house, but she'd decided to spend her own money on a hotel instead. She wasn't off her ass drunk, but definitely past the point where she ought to be driving, so she called a cab and headed outside. She shut the door behind her and breathed deeply, trying not to think of what she'd just seen or what it meant.

Even from inside the cab she could hear the music blaring and wondered how long it would be before the police were called. Maybe if they got there soon enough, Jesse wouldn't sleep with that woman.

Chapter Seven

Groaning, hands held to his head in an effort to keep it from falling off, Jesse sat up and cracked open an eye. He seemed to have fallen asleep on one of the couches in the basement, and there were other guys passed out on the floor and on the beat-up lazy boy recliner. A square of daylight through a window high on the wall revealed it to be daytime.

He pulled his phone from where it was wedged between the cushions and saw it was nearly four o'clock. Shit, he had less than an hour before they took off again. He was starving, he stunk, and he couldn't quite focus his eyes. How the hell was he going to play tonight?

This was why he'd stopped partying so hard after the last tour. It was bad for business.

Grabbing his guitar, which even in his drunken stupor he'd managed to return to its case last night, he emerged onto the first floor to find a couple guys playing video games and drinking.

"Dude, you look like shit," Kelly observed from his spot on the floor in front of the TV. "Want a beer?"

"Hell, no," Jesse said, his stomach turning over at the thought. "You've been a bad enough influence already." Grabbing his bag from the corner he headed for the bathroom.

"Not nearly bad enough," Kelly called over his shoulder, thumbs still moving on the console. "I don't know how you let that hot piece go last night. She totally wanted it."

Jesse stopped in his tracks. "What are you talking about? Do you mean Beth? Because we're–"

"Nah, not her, though now that you mention it, I'd do her too. I meant the chick that nearly sucked your face off."

"Exactly when was this?" Jesse asked, dread filling him at the thought of Beth witnessing that.

Kelly looked at him, clearly wondering why that mattered. "Dude, how the hell do I know? Sometime between you getting here and passing out."

It was starting to come back to him. Some girl kissing him just as the urgent need to take a piss had come over him. He'd untangled himself from her to find the bathroom and then wandered downstairs. He hadn't even thought of the girl again. Beth had been at the party for a while, but at some point he'd gone looking for her and come up empty. He didn't remember much after that.

Christ. Had Beth seen him kissing her?

Another groan escaped him at the sight of himself in the warped bathroom mirror. What were the chances he'd look like a human being before Beth showed up?

He hadn't shaved in days and had passed from scruffy to homeless, so he took care of that as soon as he'd showered. Maybe he was a mess and a fool, but he didn't need to give her further evidence of it.

He hadn't given up hope that he'd somehow have Beth before the end of the tour. That was the only explanation for his celibacy. He'd never gone more than a few days on the road without sex, but now he'd gone over a week with no one in his bed but him.

He couldn't stop thinking about that kiss and what might have happened if Will hadn't walked in. Would Beth have let him take her on the table? Would he have done it?

Hell, yes. He'd done worse and he'd never wanted anyone like he wanted Beth. Just remembering the feel of her mouth on his, the way she moaned and opened her legs, was making him hard again.

Maybe it was for the best they'd stopped, but he wasn't feeling particularly grateful. Certainly not to Will.

Nothing like thoughts of Will to kill his hard-on.

He emerged from the bathroom marginally more human and got himself a glass of water. Stepping outside for fresh air he found Matt and Brian tossing a Frisbee on the lawn outside.

"Oh look. It's alive," Brian cracked, throwing the Frisbee at him.

Jesse just barely made the catch. "Anyone seen Will?"

"He's still asleep upstairs," Brian said. "We were taking bets last night on which one of you would choke on your own vomit."

"I did not puke," he said, offended.

Brian raised an eyebrow but said nothing.

"Stu ran out to get greasy food and Gatorade for everyone," Matt offered. "He wants us ready to leave at five."

"That's fifteen minutes," Jesse pointed out. "Someone better wake up Will, and it's not going to be me."

Brian and Matt traded looks.

"I'll go," Brian sighed, tossing the disc to Matt.

Stu pulled up in the van a few minutes later and they sat on the steps eating and drinking Gatorade, Stu's hangover fix, not saying much. Brian returned with the news that Will was awake and starting to move. Jesse entertained the fantasy of driving away without him.

"Beth'll be here soon," Stu said between bites. "I want to hit the road as soon as she arrives. We're cutting it close as it is."

Beth's car sat parked on the street, but she'd evidently found another way to the hotel last night. He only hoped she hadn't walked. What if she'd had no way to get there and he'd been too drunk to help?

The door opened behind them and Jesse tensed instinctively at the feel of Will at his back.

"Has pretty boy told you all his little secret?" Will asked, coming down the steps. "I walked in on him practically screwing Beth in the dressing room last night."

He was pale, the dark circles shadowing his eyes giving him a haunted look, but his mouth was hard and mean.

"Shut the fuck up, Will," Jesse said, coming to his feet. "That's nobody's business."

Matt looked from him to Will, confusion and hurt written all over his face. Christ, was *everyone* in love with Beth?

"But it is," Will said, his glare unwavering. "Stu cares a lot, don't you Stu?"

Stu's voice was calm and steady. "Think about what you say, Will. We still have a lot of gigs to play. Let's finish out the tour without any more drama, okay?"

Will said nothing, just turned around and headed for the van, stowing his gear away. Jesse breathed a little easier but didn't take his eyes off the other man.

Then Will turned back and looked at Jesse. "You just have to stick in every woman you meet, don't you?"

Jesse was off the steps before he'd even had time to think about it. He shoved Will up against the van, his forearm on his throat. "Shut your mouth."

Will coughed and tried to shove him away, but Jesse was bigger and madder.

"Back off, Jesse," Stu said, his voice low. "Let me handle this."

Will wasn't sneering anymore. Fury and what appeared to be a touch of fear had him pale and shaking. Or maybe that part was the hangover. His voice was low, for Jesse's ears only when he spoke again.

"You don't even care about her. Why couldn't you just leave her alone?"

Jesse stepped away, unsure how to defend against the look of betrayal in the other man's eyes. "I do care."

Will slumped against the van. "Yeah? You have a funny way of showing it. I saw her leave after you kissed that girl last night. I'd never do that to her."

"I didn't..."

Will shot him a withering look and brushed by him. Jesse watched him, speechless, as he walked around the van and got in. No one said anything for a minute. Stu stood there grim-faced while Brian and Matt looked on as if afraid to say anything.

Jesse's head throbbed.

"Sorry I'm late!" Beth called. She was running down the sidewalk in jeans and an olive green corduroy jacket that stopped just above her ass, her computer bag on one shoulder, her suitcase rolling along behind her.

She stopped a few yards away and looked at them. "Were you waiting for me? I ended up walking all the way across town and I didn't realize how long it would take..."

She trailed off and glanced around nervously, and he could see when the realization that everyone knew hit her. Guilt flashed across her face and she bit her lip.

Jesse tensed, wondering if Stu was going to tell Matt or Brian to drive with Beth.

But Stu looked from him to Beth and sighed heavily. "Hell, you might as well get in the car. The last thing I need is you and Will in the van together."

"We were just packing up," Jesse called to Beth, his voice too loud. "You about ready to go?"

She nodded, hands clenched around her bags. "I'll drive," she said, moving around the car. She didn't look anyone in the eye, not even him.

He grabbed his bag and guitar from inside the house and put them in the car, all the while trying to ignore the looks he was getting from the guys. He'd deal with them later.

Beth pulled away from the curb and headed down the street, her face tight with tension.

"What did Stu say?" she asked, her hands white-knucking the wheel.

"Not much. He was mostly trying to keep things from getting out of hand with Will. We'll probably both hear more about it later, though."

She didn't say anything, but her misery was evident in every rigid muscle.

"Look, it was just a kiss," Jesse said. "Stu's not going to fire you over that, and the whole thing is going to blow over."

"You think Will's going to forgive and forget?" she asked, finally looking at him.

He heaved a sigh. "Well no, probably not, but he was always a pain in the ass. We'll manage.

"I just wish they didn't all know our business."

He didn't have much to say to that, and he wasn't feeling up to more conversation. The whole thing sucked. Not just being found out, but the fact that he'd finally kissed Beth and now he had to feel bad about it.

Then there was that stupid kiss last night. Christ, he couldn't even remember what she looked like.

"I don't know what you saw last night, but for the record, I didn't sleep with anyone."

"Duly noted."

She didn't look anxious to talk about it, which was fine by him. Fishing out his iPod he plugged it in and found Townes Van Zandt. If ever there was music for being hung over and bummed out, Townes was it. He closed his eyes and pretended to sleep, but he must have really dozed off, because the next thing he knew they were parked outside the club.

In a few hours he'd be up in front of another hungry crowd, whether he was ready or not.

***

Beth set up the merch table while the band got ready for soundcheck and Jesse went over the set list. Hopefully no one could tell that her nerves were scraped raw, the effort of acting normal wearing her out. Carefully she counted the cash in the lock box and inventoried the merchandise, all the while forcing herself not to look up at Jesse every five seconds.

But despite her intention to focus on work, the kiss played on a loop in her head, leaving her in a heightened state of arousal and confusion. Would it be possible to go back to the light, friendly rapport she and Jesse had managed until yesterday, or had they ruined that for good? She'd crossed a line she'd sworn not to cross, and there was no doubt she'd done some damage. The tension between Will and Jesse had been manageable before, but now? Who knew what things would be like.

She wasn't any different than the women who swooned over Jesse up on stage. They watched him, wanting what he was offering. All that achy sex, that raw animal gorgeousness. They probably imagined his tattered voice saying their name, those quick, subtle fingers skimming their skin. They wanted his intensity and his passion and his dark eyes.

She wanted all those same things, but she also had all those hours in the car talking and singing and telling stories. Even the long silences as the country revealed itself and slid away. She *knew* him, which made it all the harder. And it was only going to get worse. Singing with Jesse was almost as intimate as kissing him.

She looked up to see Stu approaching and the ball of dread expanded in her stomach.

"Does it look like we have enough of everything?" Stu asked, scanning the table.

"I think so. The last shipment should take us through the next two weeks, assuming sales are about the same as before."

"Good."

He said nothing else for a second, and she could almost see him debating whether to keep going.

"You're doing a good job," he finally said, but he was having a hard time looking at her.

"Um, thanks." She took a deep breath. "I don't know what Will said, but it was just–"

"Look, I'm not going to fire you, though the thought had crossed my mind. But frankly the last thing I need is Jesse flipping out on me. I'd never hear the end of it, and it would just make my life harder. But that doesn't mean I won't do it if things get any worse. I do *not* want any more of the shit I had to deal with this morning."

The guys were plugging in about twenty yards away. All of them looked tense and tired, but they moved through the routine like they did every night. Jesse looked over at her and Stu, frowning, and she prayed silently he wouldn't come over.

"It won't happen again," she choked out.

Stu sighed, clearly unhappy about having the conversation. "You and Jesse have a nice thing going, and you're bringing out great things in him and his music. He can be a real sweetheart, but he only cares about one thing. Just remember that. Everything but his music is a diversion. Right now it's easy. He doesn't have to make any tough choices. But soon you'll be gone and he'll still be doing this. And I don't have to tell you there are always other girls."

She was having trouble breathing, but she wasn't going to let him know that.

"I know, I just...things got carried away," she said, but instead of looking at him, which was impossible without revealing her struggle, she stared at the inventory sheet on the table. "It won't happen again."

"It's my fault. I saw this coming but I hired you anyway. I'm not entirely sorry, though. Not yet, anyway. But girls never refuse Jesse. No one does, come to that. I shouldn't have expected you to be different."

Her head snapped up. "I'm not like *every girl*," she said, slamming the cash box closed with a loud clang. "If I were, he'd have had me on my back the first night. I also happen to be doing a better job than anyone else you'll ever get. Now, can I get on with my job, please?"

A raised eyebrow was his only reaction. "Why yes, you can. I think we're done here."

Beth said nothing, just waited for him to leave. As soon as he'd gone she slumped into the chair, the cold metal nothing compared to the chill that had taken over her. Jesus, talk about a reality check. It wasn't like she'd been deluding herself, but leave it to Stu to put a fine point on it. Then again, he knew Jesse, and nothing he said had been designed to hurt her. Stu was only looking out for Jesse, the band, and her. In that order.

He'd also purposefully provoked her, if she wasn't mistaken.

She sat there alternating between seething anger and wrenching guilt, but she didn't have the luxury of wallowing. There was too much to do. Besides, if she was going to slip up, that scorching kiss was the way to do it. This diversion from real life was going to be over in two weeks, and then she'd go back to Las Vegas and the job hunt and make a life for herself. A life that set her free rather than constrained her. Spending these weeks with Jesse was good exercise for the way she wanted to be. He knew what he wanted and didn't let anything get in his way. He didn't take any crap, and neither would she.

Her inner pep talk perked her up enough that she felt ready when Jesse called her up for a quick rehearsal. She wasn't going to just get on stage because he'd talked her into it, she was going because she wanted to. Because it was fun and she was good at it.

She smiled at everyone as she took her place next to Jesse. Matt and Brian gave wan smiles. Will looked away.

She'd almost suggested to Jesse that they skip the song tonight, but she knew him well enough to predict his reaction to that. Now she was glad. It felt good to be up there, even if she wasn't entirely welcome.

"Did Stu give you a hard time?" Jesse asked.

"It was nothing," she said, adjusting the microphone. "Just the usual."

He didn't look convinced but let it go and called out to the sound guy. It was more or less the same as last night, except she came in on time, and she was less tentative. In fact she was raring to go, energy bursting from her seams. Last night she'd been ready to let Jesse lead her anywhere, today she was right there beside him.

When it was over he gave her a little smile, his head tilted like he was trying to figure her out.

"That was real good."

She just smiled. She hadn't done anything on purpose, but she felt different and it changed the way she sang.

"I'm going to make a call and then find something to eat," she said, hopping off the stage, "I'll see you in a couple hours."

Jesse looked taken aback, probably because she always ate with the band, but there was no rule that said she had to do that. Besides, the way they were all at each other's throats, a little space wasn't such a bad idea.

Back outside she sat in her car and called Cheryl.

"Finally!" her friend answered. "I was beginning to wonder if I'd ever hear from you again. The only reason I know you're alive is all your tweets."

"That's about all there is to know." She paused. "Well, that and I kissed Jesse last night."

Cheryl's squeal would have done a thirteen year-old girl proud. "Oh my God, tell me everything. Was it amazing?"

"It was the hottest thing that's ever happened to me, hands down. Then Will walked in and it went downhill from there. Everybody seems to have an opinion about it and I feel like I have a scarlet letter stitched on my shirt, but it's kind of an interesting feeling to be the bad girl."

"But why does this guy Will care? I mean, it's a band. Aren't they all screwing everything that moves, anyway?"

"Pretty much. But Will seems to have a thing for me, or he did anyway. Plus he's jealous of all the attention Jesse gets."

"So what happens now?"

"We just keep doing what we've been doing, but without the kissing."

"You think you guys can manage all the heat?"

Beth let out a groan. "We'll have to. I can't be the reason this tour falls apart. Stu gave me this whole talking to that kind of put me in my place."

"That jerk."

"He was kind of a jerk, but he was just doing what he had to. I did mess up. But it's not all bad. I got a smoking hot kiss out of the deal, so at least I have a benchmark now."

"Well that's something. But you shouldn't get all the blame. You weren't the only one there."

"I have a feeling Stu's had words with Jesse, but it's more complicated for them. Jesse's the talent, and Stu's dedicated to him. Stu expected Jesse to hit on me, and he expected me to keep him out of my pants."

Cheryl gave a snort. "You're only human. I'm surprised you lasted this long."

She was about to take offense, but instead she sighed. "Me too. But I think I've got a grip now. And I'll still be singing with him. That's almost as good as messing around with him."

"I still can't believe you're performing. I'm coming to one of your shows, you know."

"The closest we'll be to you is Flagstaff on the eighth. That's a Saturday."

"Perfect! We'll make it a road trip."

"I'll get you and Jason tickets for that one. Let me know if I should get some for Emily and Cutter, too."

"Will do. I can't wait."

"But enough about me. How are things with you? Has your class settled down?"

"I've still got a couple troublemakers, but nothing I can't handle. I just wish I were taller so I could tower over the boys like Jason does."

"Yeah, I bet. A little intimidation goes a long way." She laughed, a memory resurfacing. "Remember how you waited and waited for your growth spurt all through high school? It wasn't until you were eighteen that you finally accepted you weren't going to grow anymore."

"I know. I was so jealous of you."

"Oh, please. For years no one would date me, but you were always cute as a button."

"Trust me, you didn't miss out on anything."

"So how's Mr. Right, anyway? You keeping him in line?"

"I guess I must be. He proposed to me last night."

"Oh my God. Tell me everything."

"It's kind of a funny story, actually. We hiked to this spot he knows, Chapel Ledge, and when we got there he started telling me how great I am, how much he loves me, that kind of stuff." Cheryl started to laugh, her breath hitching as she tried to get the words out. "But I was barely listening. I was starving and all I could think about was getting to the spot so we could have our little picnic.

"Cheryl, no."

"So he asked me if I'd heard anything he said, and I said I'd gotten the gist."

Beth was laughing so hard she could barely speak. "Oh my God. Poor Jason."

"So he rolls his eyes at me, takes his backpack off and pulls out this little box." Cheryl's voice was hitching again, but this time it wasn't laughter. "He said he'd try to be more obvious, and then he got down on one knee and..."

Beth waited through her sniffling until she was calm enough to talk again.

"He said all kinds of romantic stuff, and by that point I was listening pretty hard, but my knees wouldn't hold me so I sort of collapsed next to him and told him yes."

"Mazel tov, honey. I'm so happy for you."

Beth was full-on crying now, her heart swelling with happiness for Cheryl. If anyone deserved this, it was her.

"We haven't set a date, but you can be sure I'll be keeping you apprised of every single detail. I have to say, it's very convenient of you to move to town in time for me to be bridezilla."

"Bring it, sister."

"I probably should let you go so you can get ready for tonight."

"Yeah. I'll call you soon, though."

Beth was still teary when she got out of the car. She scrubbed at her face and hoped she wouldn't look all red and blotchy when it was time to go on tonight.

"Beth? What's wrong?"

She looked up to see Jesse rushing toward her. Before she could form a sentence he had his hands on her shoulders and was staring down at her, the look in his eyes pure panic.

"Why are you crying? Was it something Stu said?"

"Take it easy. It's nothing like that."

His posture eased a bit, but he didn't take his hands off her. "So everything's okay? You're not leaving?"

"What? No, of course not." She side-stepped the issue of what Stu had said to her. "My best friend just told me she's engaged and I'm…I'm just happy for her. She's been through so much and now she has this great guy." Her tears started up again, which meant it was only a matter of time before her nose started running, too. "I would have bet anything he was the guy. It was so obvious when I saw them together, but somehow hearing it from her is making me fall apart."

Jesse pulled a red handkerchief out of his back pocket. God, she loved that he carried these things around. It was so old school it was cool. Or maybe she just thought that because she liked him so much. Maybe it was really old-mannish and she was just too blinded by her pheromones to see that.

She wiped her eyes and dabbed at her nose, praying she didn't look too gross. Jesse had stepped back a bit and was no longer touching her, but he still looked worried. "Are you upset because you didn't get married?"

"I'm just happy for her. We grew up together and she lived with my family for a few years." She shrugged, unable to explain it exactly. "This is the best news I've ever gotten."

She smiled, touched that he cared enough to worry. From what she knew of him, and of men in general, feelings weren't his MO. Unless he was singing, that is. As she watched his expression changed, his eyes moving over her face like he was trying to take her all in. Then one hand came up to cup her cheek, his thumb brushing away a tear.

She stopped breathing, caught by the hungry, tender look she saw there. He'd run toward her because he'd thought she was upset, thought she was leaving, even.

She took a step back and his hand dropped away. "I'd better get going. I'm starving, and I still need to change and warm up."

His look was long and assessing, then he nodded, as if sensing she wanted some time alone. She backed up a few steps, still facing him, then turned and walked out of the parking lot and down the street, smiling to herself.

Chapter Eight

Jesse watched Beth walk away, everything in him wanting to follow her. Which was why he didn't.

He and Stu went to a diner a few blocks away, leaving the other guys to do their own thing. The band was splintering, but he didn't feel like doing much about it. Maybe he should have tried harder with Will once he realized he had a crush on Beth. It might have made a difference, but he'd never know now.

"Margaret called. She's got a good offer for you to contribute a song to a movie soundtrack."

"Oh yeah? What kind of movie?"

His agent had been fielding a lot of offers lately, some good, some not so good. He tried not to get too caught up in any of it while on tour, but he couldn't deny that having people come to him was a nice change.

"An indie western. That's how they're pitching it, anyway. The money's just okay, but the producer is top-notch and there's potential for strong soundtrack sales. She'll be sending you details."

Jesse nodded and bit into his burger. He chewed for a few seconds. "I think you're right about not moving labels. Terry's been good to me and the deal looks fair. Plus we can record wherever we want."

"It's all coming together, Jesse. Just keep your eye on the ball and it'll only get better."

Was Stu talking about Beth? Just because he thought about her all the damn time didn't mean he was going to screw up his career.

"Do you have some reason to think I'm taking my eye off it?"

"All I meant was, this is it, right here. It's all happening just like we planned, and it's my job to help you bring it home."

"Fine. But your job doesn't include reaming Beth out."

"Is that what she said I did?"

"She didn't say anything, but I saw you talking to her."

"I just reminded her what I expected from someone in her position. She's a great girl and I get what you see in her, but you're going to be saying goodbye before long. She likes you too much already. Don't make it harder than it has to be."

Jesse bit back a retort, aware he was treading on thin ice. Stu had mountains of patience with his foibles, but the strain of the last few days was clearly wearing on him. He should have kept his mouth shut and not brought Beth into it.

Stu deftly turned the conversation to talk of the forthcoming album, and by the time they left the diner his head was full of ideas about who to get in to produce and play. But for some reason he kept picturing Beth in the studio with him, recording "Better Off."

Back in the club he entered the bathroom just as Will was leaving. They walked by each other without exchanging a word, though that was no different than before Will had walked in on him and Beth.

Quickly he changed into a fresh shirt and studied his reflection – skin nicked near his mouth and under his chin from shaving with a shaky hand this morning, dark circles under his eyes. He was feeling better than he had earlier in the day, but he still looked like shit. It wouldn't matter, though. Up on stage he'd still look like something. What amazed him was how the girls came at him after every show, no matter how sweaty or drunk he was.

But girls screamed and went crazy over almost any guy swinging a guitar. An instrument made everyone look good, provided you could play even a little. He kind of got it, actually. When he saw a musician he loved, part of him wanted to be that person, or somehow take away what they had, bottle the experience. If it was a woman, he wanted to sleep with her, like he could absorb her talent and the feeling she brought out in him. He'd slept with a couple women he'd felt that way about while watching them perform, but the feeling had never translated into the sex.

Then there was Beth. He'd wanted to sleep with her since he met her, but now that they sang together, her sweet, husky voice pulled that same desire from him. He just wanted to go to wherever her songs lived and stay there.

He found the rest of the guys and Stu in the green room and sat down with a nod to the room in general. He took out the set list and looked it over. Did he want to keep "Short End of the Stick" in the last set? It was kind of a downer. Maybe better to do it earlier in the night.

He saw her red boots first.

Slowly he lifted his gaze, his pulse an erratic bass line as he took in her long legs. She was wearing a new pair of tight dark jeans and a lacey black top that allowed her skin to peek through all the tiny holes. The only thing keeping her from being ex-rated was a red camisole the exact same color as her lips.

But Christ, those boots.

"Hot damn, Beth," Matt said, a dopey grin on his face. "You are *smokin'*. Where've you been hiding those boots?"

She was blushing, her smile uncertain. "I just bought them. You don't think it's too much?"

"Hell, no. God meant for you to wear that exact thing tonight."

Jesus, now Matt was actually being kind of charming.

"You look real nice," Jesse said, finally opening his own trap. Hoping to divert her attention back to him. It actually *hurt* to watch her look at another guy.

Pathetic.

She smiled right at him before looking away, and her flush deepened and spread down her neck. She'd flushed exactly that way when they'd kissed, and the urge to haul her off somewhere so she could wrap her legs around him, boots and all, speared through him with such intensity he stopped breathing.

"Dude, stop looking at her like that," Matt muttered, playing a few discordant notes on his guitar for emphasis.

Right. Stop looking at her like that. He could do that. If he stopped looking at her altogether.

He bent over the set list again, his teeth clamped over a pick as he watched her from the corner of his eye. She surveyed the room as if to decide where it was safest to sit before falling onto the couch next to Brian and taking a deep pull from the beer he handed her.

Jesse watched her swallow and remembered the salt he'd licked from her throat.

The opening band came in from doing their soundcheck and provided a welcome distraction for everyone, though Jesse could have lived without those guys staring at Beth, too. She disappeared a little while later, probably to warm-up, and he tried to give a shit about what the other guys were saying.

Then the opening band went on, which meant Beth was already manning the merch table. He was increasingly annoyed she had to do that, but he wasn't about to broach it with Stu. He'd just get an earful about how that's what she'd been hired for, blah blah blah.

The sold-out crowd was going nuts when Jesse got out there. Unlike the other gigs they'd played recently, the energy in the room was edgy, as if everyone was ready to hit the ceiling. Which he liked to a point, but he'd have to control things tonight so they didn't ruin the vibe.

Beth had become his touchstone during performances, and tonight was no different. Seeing her out there was enough to pull more from him than he thought he had left. He was already geared up from seeing her before he went on and he was playing his heart out, like he had to prove something to her. Like if he played well enough she'd give in and let him have her.

She was temptation itself out there, the black lace slipping over her skin, her silky hair sliding over her eye. Every so often she tossed her head and he thought he'd have a heart attack. Some part of his brain, the part connected to his dick, thought she was already his.

He was impatient to call her up on stage, but the anticipation gave the songs before it the pleasurable tension of foreplay. He walked the line between want and satisfaction, pleasure and desperation, until his whole body thrummed like a plucked guitar string.

The first set went fine, though he could have done without some of the yelling during his quieter songs. But he didn't let it get to him. In the early days with Buddy's band, he'd played hellholes that made this look like a walk in the park.

Finally it was time to call her up and she made her way through the crowd and up onto the stage, smiling and graceful, an old pro already. He took her hand as she climbed the stairs and came to stand beside him, her energy thrilling up his arm. Gone were the anxiety and terror from before. She was smiling at him, telling him she was ready.

"Ya'all give it up for Beth Levine, chanteuse extraordinaire," he exhorted the crowd, and for a few seconds the room was deafening.

Then they started to sing and the crowd quieted except for a few scattered shouts and whistles. Turning his body so that he could face both her and the audience, he sang to her and watched her beautiful face as she sang back the lyrics he'd written, lyrics she'd already made her own.

Every time she sang them she did it a little bit different, and tonight he heard something new again. Listening to her he realized other possibilities in it, even in the way he thought about the women who'd inspired it. But that revelation was nothing to the revelation of her standing mere inches from him. She was radiant, her face flushed, her eyes alive and expressive. He'd never seen anyone more beautiful. And she was as out of reach off stage as she was on.

Then the song was over, much as he would have liked it to go on forever, and she headed back to her spot by the table, the crowd parting for her like she was royalty. The people she passed smiled, their eyes shining. Some of them reached out to touch her.

***

"I'm going to miss these drives," Beth said, her voice wistful.

They were a couple hours into their drive to Jackson, Wyoming, and Jesse was already wishing the drive were longer. The car was the only place he had Beth to himself.

"Oh yeah? I'd have thought by now you'd be sick of all this," he said.

She took her eyes off the road to look at him. "Me? No way. This is exactly why I took the job."

"Next time around it's going to be different. Stu's already looking into a tour bus. It'll be like the circus coming to town."

"A bus, really?"

"Yeah, with beds and TVs, a bar. You wouldn't believe what they put on those things." He smiled at her, already feeling nostalgic. "But I'll miss this. Just you and me in a car, going places."

"But it'll mean you've made it," she said, and her voice was soft, a little huskier. "You have to be glad about that. It's what you've always wanted."

"It is. But it's not the only thing I want."

He felt her glance at him but didn't meet her eye. As happy as he was being with her, he couldn't shake the melancholy that had come over him while writing that morning. Part of it was where the song had taken him, but it was also the end of the tour looming in the distance, getting closer with every mile.

Not that he wanted to be on the road forever. He'd been touring nearly non-stop for three months already, and even he had his limits. He was also getting anxious to start recording his new album. But he wasn't sure he was ready for all the changes coming at him. He definitely knew he didn't want to say goodbye to Beth.

"What do you think about trying another song? I've been working on this duet," he said, reaching back and grabbing his guitar.

"You want me to sing another song with you? Like onstage?"

"Sure. Everybody loves you." Maybe this was his way of getting more of her, but if he couldn't have sex with her, he was going to sing with her as much as possible. "I'll sing both parts the first time through so you get the idea."

He took off his seatbelt to get a better angle with the guitar. Beth bit her lip like she was dying to say something about safety, and Jesse had to look out the window for a few seconds to hide his smile. She was so adorable she just about killed him.

When he looked back he was all business. He played it through once, then the second time she came in and sang her part. The song had an old time swing to it and the lyrics he'd written were pretty and they rhymed, so Beth picked them up quickly. She'd even put the car in cruise control so she could tap her toe.

"So what do you think?" he asked when they'd finished.

"It's a great song. Let's practice it a couple more days at soundcheck. If it comes together, I'm in."

"Perfect. I want to have a few new tunes for Austin, especially since there'll be a lot of folks there who've heard me before."

"So you'll stay in Austin after this?" she asked.

"Yeah, that's been home base for the last few years. There are tons of great musicians and studios, so I should have no trouble putting together some kick-ass sessions. We're already lining things up for when I get back."

"I can't wait to see it. I hear it's a great city."

"Stick around and I can show you around myself," he said, putting the guitar back.

Her eyes went wide in surprise and she flushed, like she'd just thought about what they might do together once the tour was over.

"We'll see," was all she said.

He didn't say more, partly because he didn't want to overdo it, partly because his own invitation had surprised him. Messing around on tour while there were limits was one thing, but inviting her to stay in town with him afterward was different. Potentially messier.

"I like the boots," he said, suddenly aware he hadn't said a word about them. "They suit you."

He felt her smile, warm and pleased even before she spoke.

"You're right. They do."

He looked at her then, drinking in the soft, happy smile, the way her hair waved over her eye, the effect so sexy he wanted to howl. Why couldn't she have a shitty personality, or be less sexy? Why did she have to be the whole package?

"What'll you do when the tour's over?" he asked.

He'd been avoiding all talk about after the tour, but he couldn't keep his head in the sand forever.

"I'll go back to Las Vegas. It's not exactly home yet, but Cheryl's there, and it seems like as good a place as any to start over. Stu told me he'll be getting a business manager for you. I looked into what that was, and it actually sounds kind of cool."

"You mean you want to be my business manager?"

"Well, not yours. But I could do it for other bands once I got up and running. Most business managers are accountants, so I have that going for me. And I've had a front row seat to a lot of the things a band deals with. It kind of seems like the perfect thing. I just have to figure out how to get started."

"Huh, sounds cool," was all he said.

She smiled, her eyes lighting up. "I can see myself working with musicians to improve the business side of things. I'd be good at it, and I'll care. That's the thing I've been looking for. I just didn't know what it was going to be until now."

"I can already tell you'll be great at it," he said, but he couldn't seem to muster the right amount of enthusiasm, even though he meant it.

She'd be great at that kind of thing. He just couldn't help wondering why she was so quick to say she wouldn't do it for him. He almost asked but couldn't bring himself to do it. What if he didn't like the answer? They stopped soon after for lunch. As soon as they ordered Beth pulled out a handful of brochures on tourist attractions.

"So, we'll be passing Grand Tetons National Park, Yellowstone, and a bunch of other national parks. Pretty much the whole state is a national park, but I've always wanted to see Yellowstone."

"That is why you made me get up at nine o'clock this morning. So yeah, let's do it. It's only," he looked at his phone, "twelve-thirty. We should be there by two-thirty, so we'll still have plenty of daylight."

She beamed at him, her smile so full of joy it stopped his breath.

"Now aren't you glad I made you get up so early?" she said, taking one of the fries off his plate and dipping it into his ketchup. "The guys won't have time to see anything."

"We'll see," he said, purposefully sounding noncommittal.

She didn't need to know he only did it to make her happy. If he hadn't been with her, he wouldn't have cared if he saw a park. Only Beth could make him choose some natural wonder over sleep.

They ate quickly and headed out, Jesse at the wheel while Beth looked up visiting information on her phone.

"The interior roads are closed now, but Mammoth Hot Springs in right inside the north entrance. We can at least see that."

Dark clouds were piling up in the rearview mirror as he drove east, but it looked like they'd have time to see the park and get to the city before any weather hit. More than anything he wanted to see that look of joy on Beth's face again. He was beginning to think he'd do just about anything to give it to her.

Beth insisted on paying the entrance fee, but since he was in the driver's seat he was able to fend her off and pay it himself.

"You didn't have to do that. This was my idea," she said, exasperated.

He couldn't tell her this felt like the closest thing to a date he'd ever get with her, so he just shrugged and said nothing. He parked the car and they dug around in their bags for warmer shoes and clothes. It wasn't much over forty degrees and it seemed to be dropping fast. He pulled on a pair of beat-up hiking books and a down vest, then turned around to find Beth in a fur-lined pair of boots, a down jacket and red hat and gloves. Where she'd managed to stash it all this time, he had no clue.

He laughed. "Well, at least one of us is prepared."

The hot springs weren't what he expected. He'd pictured water spraying out of a few holes, but instead it sort of seeped out of different terrace formations, some of them multi-colored. Jupiter Terrace actually looked like it could have been on a different planet.

They followed the path from one terrace to another, the heat from the springs warming them somewhat. But gradually the temperature fell and Beth started shivering.

"You're freezing," he said, laying his bare hand against her cheek.

She yelped and gave a little hop. "I'm a little cold, but your hands are like ice cubes. Don't you have a hat and gloves?"

"I didn't bring any with me. I'll find something tomorrow. It's no big deal."

"We might as well go. They'll probably close it down soon, anyway."

They hadn't seen anyone besides rangers since they arrived. Maybe that was with good reason. They hurried back to the car and he blasted the heat as soon as it had warmed up.

"Thank you for doing this," she said, her voice soft and drowsy.

She'd finally stopped shivering and looked like she might fall asleep.

"I wouldn't have missed it for anything."

He meant a lot more than the park, but she didn't have to know that.

***

Beth dropped her bags on the floor and fell into bed, the late night and long drive finally catching up with her. She'd agreed to meet Jesse in the bar for dinner at seven, which meant she had an hour to nap. She left the curtains open and drifted off as the first snowflakes fell.

When her alarm woke her up it was snowing hard. No message from Stu, though. Did that mean they were still out in this? She tried calling him, then Matt and Brian, but it just rang and rang, eventually going to their voicemail. Either something horrible had happened or they didn't have reception. Or both.

Jesse was already waiting for her in the bar when she came down.

"Have you heard from Stu?" she asked him.

"No, I was just going to ask you the same thing. But I'm sure it's fine. If they left at noon and stopped to eat, they would just be getting here now. Let's give it more time before we freak out. Maybe they pulled off somewhere."

He was only trying to make them both feel better so she didn't argue. Maybe he was right. With all the tourist attractions in the area there were more motels than you'd normally find in such a rural area. They could have pulled off at one of them. But wouldn't Stu have called if that were the case?

They ordered their food, but she was too anxious to sit still so she excused herself and headed into the lobby. There she stood at the front doors peering out into blowing snow and darkness, the thought of them all out there turning her skin clammy. She'd just begun to pray silently for their safe return when a more solid whiteness materialized in the parking lot. Straining her eyes, as if that would help her penetrate the storm, she stood and stared until Stu, Matt, Brian and Will formed out of the blowing snow and came toward her.

"Oh my God, you made it," she said, throwing her arms around Stu's neck. "I was so worried about you guys."

He stopped in surprise, then gave a tired smile. "So were we."

"Jesse and I were just about to eat, if you guys want to join us."

"Hell yeah, I'm starving," Matt said, rubbing his hands together to get warm.

They were all underdressed and shivering.

"Why don't you guys check in and meet us down in the bar," she said, suddenly wanting the whole gang together.

They gave varying sounds of agreement and headed to the front desk, but Beth put her hand on Will's arm.

"Can I talk to you for a second?" she asked.

His whole body tensed and he refused to look her in the eye, but he stayed. The guys glanced back at them with varying degrees of curiosity and worry, but at least they left them alone.

She took a deep breath. "I just wanted to say I'm sorry about everything."

He looked at her then, his skin flushed, dark eyes intense. "I thought you were smarter than to fall for that guy. I saw you leave after he kissed that woman at the party. How could you be into someone who does that right after kissing you?"

He had a point, even if Jesse hadn't done anything with that particular woman. But she wasn't in the mood to answer to Will.

"I appreciate your concern, but you hardly know me," she said, trying not to sound too harsh. "I think this might have more to do with how much you resent Jesse."

His head snapped back like she'd slapped him. "No. It's not about that."

"Jesse and I hit it off. I like him, and I won't apologize for that, but I'm really sorry we took it too far." She hugged her arms to her chest, partly to ward off the chill from the door, partly to ward off Will's agitation. "You and Jesse need each other, Will. I think you should forget about me and try to see the bigger picture."

He stared at her like he didn't know what to say, then his whole body seemed to sag a little. When he finally spoke he sounded sad and tired. "I guess I can try."

That was more than she'd expected. He looked defeated, but that was better than the barely suppressed fury he'd been walking around with.

"You must be hungry," she said. "Why don't you check in so you can meet us for dinner."

He nodded and picked his bass and duffel bag back up, walking away without a word.

Jesse looked up when she came back to the table.

"They're all here, safe and sound. They should be down soon to join us," she said, leaving out her conversation with Will. She didn't feel like talking that one over.

He looked as relieved as she felt. Probably he'd been freaking just as hard as her, but being a guy he'd hidden it. Their food came a minute later, the rest of the band shortly thereafter. Everyone looked tired, but marginally better than when they'd arrived.

Will sat down at the end opposite from Jesse, and he didn't look thrilled, but at least he was there.

"So what happened to you guys?" Beth asked, moving over to let Stu in. "We were imagining the worst."

"It almost was the worst," Brian muttered, sitting down on her other side.

"No shit," Matt said, falling into a chair. His face was red, his hair standing up in tufts all over his head. "I thought we were gonna crash and die. And even before I thought we were gonna crash, the heater broke and I thought we were gonna freeze to death."

That started everyone talking about how the heater went, then the snow started and Stu could barely see even as the van slid all over the road.

"I was just lucky I saw the turn into town," Stu added. He looked even more worn-out than usual and he still shivered even though the bar was over-warm. "I don't know what I was thinking coming through here this time of year."

On a normal day everyone would have been giving him a hard time, but no one did. Which just showed how shaken up they all were. The animosity that had been in the air for so long was gone, and even Will was starting to look less tense.

They all ordered huge amounts of food and plenty of alcohol, eating and drinking until they were full and heavy.

"I feel so guilty," Beth said, taking a sip of her Irish coffee. "We beat the storm, and my heater worked. We even stopped for a little while at Yellowstone and saw Mammoth Hot Springs."

Matt snorted. "I'd still take the near death experience over getting up at nine in the morning."

That cracked everyone up.

Stu gave a low groan and leaned back to let the waitress take his plate. "I got the final cut of the video Drobak put together for me."

"Yeah? How's it look?" Jesse asked.

"I don't know, I haven't watched it yet. You can come take a look if you want."

"I want to see, too," Matt said, sounding like a little kid afraid of being left out.

"What video?" Beth asked.

"I asked a friend to shoot some footage of the band about a month ago. I thought it'd be good to have some live video for promo stuff."

"That's a great," Beth said, leaning forward. "You can put it on your website. You should have your own YouTube channel, too."

Stu nodded. "Not a bad idea." He looked around the table. "Anyone who wants to see it can come back to my room."

Stu paid the check and got up and they all followed after him. Even Will, after a brief hesitation.

The few other people who'd been in the bar had long since left and the inn seemed deserted. They trooped together to Stu's room a couple floors up and piled onto the king-sized bed. Beth sat on the rickety desk chair. She had to lean to the side to see Stu's laptop, but that was a small price to pay to avoid all those male body parts.

It was good footage, better than other live video she's seen of them. The band was tight, and Jesse was as charismatic as usual, working the crowd, singing his heart out.

"I remember that night," Matt said, moving closer. "See that sweet piece of ass in the front? She came backstage after the show and gave me a–"

Jesse shoved Matt so that he fell into Brian.

"Dude, what the–" Matt started, then looked over at Beth. "Oh, sorry, Beth."

"Don't worry about it," she said, amused. "You guys sound great. This is the perfect way to get some of the excitement of your shows across."

"Speaking of which, I've got a new song I want Beth to try one of these nights," Jesse said. "It's called 'Down by the River.'"

Everyone, Stu and Will included, seemed to take this in stride.

"Why don't we run through it now," Matt said. "We don't have anything else to do."

Jesse looked over at her. "What do you think?"

"Sure. The more practice I get, the better."

"Get your guitars and do it in here then," Stu said. He was doing something on his phone, but he looked up and caught Jesse's surprised expression. "What? I want to hear it, too."

"Why don't you get the mandolin," Jesse said to Matt, and they left the room together, Will at their heels.

Brian fell back on the bed and appeared to doze. He couldn't play drums in the hotel, and sleeping seemed to be his next favorite activity.

Soon everyone was back in the room, tuning up and talking it through. Brian opened his eyes and offered a comment every so often. Beth mostly listened. The atmosphere in the room was so different from what it had been since she arrived on tour, but especially since

Will walked in on her and Jesse. There was a camaraderie she'd never seen before, and she only hoped it lasted.

Maybe her talk with Will had really done some good, or maybe it had taken a near-death experience to bring them together. But now she was a part of it, for the moment at least.

Jesse played his acoustic guitar, Matt the mandolin, and Will played his bass unplugged. If there had been anyone in the adjoining rooms they probably wouldn't have been too thrilled, but the hotel seemed pretty empty.

Jesse talked Matt and Will through the song first. Once they had their parts down she came in. She flubbed it several times during the first run-through, but the guys were patient with her, letting her take her time. By the fourth run-through her voice felt good, like she could sing all night.

Stu recorded bits and pieces on his phone, moving around the room for different angles.

"Another soundcheck or two and I think we've got it," Jesse said, smiling at Beth.

This time she didn't hem and haw. "I think so, too."

His grin grew bigger. Then he was playing again, but this time it was the "Dukes of Hazard" theme song, which she'd only recently learned was written by Jesse's hero, Waylon Jennings. Will and Matt grinned and joined in like they knew it by heart.

They moved from that to Johnny Cash, Charlie Rich, and early Elvis. Mostly she listened, but sometimes she knew the words, and when she did she couldn't help but sing.

Then someone knocked on the door, bringing everyone to a sudden halt. Beth glanced at the clock and was shocked to see it was after midnight. Stu opened the door to a young hotel employee in a rumpled white shirt and dark tie.

"I'm sorry sir, but I'm going to have to ask you to stop playing." He looked nervously around at everyone. "We've had complaints from the room above you."

Stu made his apologies, assuring the man they'd stop. He shut the door and looked around. "All right, party's over."

"Wanna hit the bar again?" Jesse asked the room in general.

Stu and Beth declined, but the guys were all for it, even Brian. Apparently his nap had given him a second wind.

"I'll see you boys tomorrow," Beth said, getting up.

She left the room to a chorus of "'night, Beth," and smiled all the way to her room.

Chapter Nine

After Jackson they played Salt Lake City, then left for Flagstaff, still debating whether to stop at Bryce Canyon, Zion National Park, or the Grand Canyon on the way.

"I've never been to the Grand Canyon," Beth said. "We have to stop there."

"It's not that I don't want to," Jesse said, stowing his bags in the car. "I'm just saying maybe it's best to leave it for when you've got more time. We have half a day, and that's really not enough to see much."

She handed him a coffee and muffin, mulling it over. Once again he'd gotten up extra early so they'd have time to stop and sightsee, so she couldn't complain. It was more that there was so much to see and not enough time to do it. What if she never got another chance to come back this way? And even if she did come back again, it wouldn't be with Jesse.

"You'll see it some other time," he said, as if reading her thoughts. Or some of them, anyway. "Now that you're in Vegas there'll be nothing to it."

"So what do you suggest?"

"Zion's beautiful, in fact I like it better than the Grand Canyon, but it's better if you have a couple days to see it. Bryce is amazing, and you can see it in a few hours."

Beth acquiesced, still wishing she could see it all. But even with that night off, there was no way to do more. So Jesse took the wheel and they headed south on highway fifteen, stopping once at a gas station in the middle of miles of nearly barren landscape. Beth pumped gas while Jesse stretched beside her. They had their routine down now, a place for everything in the car, a system to how they picked the music.

"It's so empty out here," she said, looking around at the rocky land on all sides, the mountain ridges breaking the skyline here and there. "I still haven't gotten used to it."

"It's pretty great, though, isn't it? Gives you space to think."

"You're right, it does. I wonder if I'll miss it when this is over."

"I will," Jesse said. "As much as I love Austin, I need to get out of the city every so often."

"That's how I felt in Gulliver. Not that it's a big city, but there's lots of farmland around it. I used to go for long drives in the countryside to clear my head. Especially right before I moved."

"Nothing like a relationship going bad to get you on the road," Jesse said, looking like he'd been there himself.

She put the gas cap back on and went inside to pay and use the bathroom. Jesse came back to the counter with Smartfood and M&Ms, her two favorites. After so many days on the road together, they knew each other's preferences and peccadilloes. He knew her better than anyone but Cheryl, which made it all the harder to imagine saying goodbye.

***

"It's like we're on another planet," Beth said, her eyes wide in amazement.

They were at the bottom of Bryce Canyon, surrounded by formations of red rock carved by wind and water. Some looked like giant chess pieces in the middle of a game, some like castles, others like nothing else on earth.

Pulling out his phone, he took pictures of her peering up at the formations, her eyes bright with amazement.

"Hey, what are you doing?" she asked, catching him in the act.

"Just taking a couple pictures. Maybe I'll put them on Facebook."

He hadn't actually been planning to do that, but it seemed like a good excuse. Better than telling her he wanted to be able to see her face after she was gone.

"No one wants to see me up there."

"Sure they do. You're the big mystery."

"Let's keep it a mystery, then. They only care about me because they think I'm sleeping with you."

As soon as the words were out she bit her lip like she regretted saying anything. He should have been good and kept his mouth shut, let the moment pass, but he couldn't stop himself.

"Maybe. Too bad they're not right."

He let that sink in before turning away, like he found something fascinating to look at. The canyon had amazed him the first time he saw it, and it did this time, too. But it was Beth that blew his mind. Beth he couldn't stop looking at.

He caught up with her a few minutes later and they pretended nothing had happened. That was his life now, acting like he wasn't burning alive.

She held the phone up and snapped a picture of him. "There, I posted it with a note about the show tomorrow."

"You really think anyone cares about me sightseeing?"

She gave him a look. "Jesse, people love this kind of thing. It makes them feel like they know you. Besides, all the women are in love with you and want to know everything. If you ever looked at your page you'd see what I mean."

"I did look once, and it was terrifying," he said.

"Someone's going to need to do it when I'm gone."

He hated when she said things like that. "We'd better get going," he said, heading toward the trail out of the canyon.

She insisted on driving the rest of the way to Flagstaff, so he pulled out his notebook and worked on some songs. He wanted to go into the recording sessions with more material than he needed in case some songs didn't work. He was still obsessing over one lyric when the light started to go. Looking out his window he caught the sunset burning up the western sky.

Beth's face was serene in the warm light, a little smile playing at the corners of her mouth. Gone was the clenched two-handed grip she used to keep on the steering wheel. One hand rested loosely on the wheel, the other tapped out a rhythm on her thigh as she sang along with Gillian Welch. She was still hitting the gas, too. He watched as the speedometer needle crept higher, topping ninety.

He'd never been one to tell a woman to slow down, and he wasn't about to start now. Not when she'd finally forgotten to worry and was flying down the highway like a woman set free.

She'd changed since that first day. She was more sure of herself, easier in her skin. She didn't seem to be trying to disappear anymore, either. Along the way she'd picked up new clothes to wear while performing, and they were sexier and flashier than what she'd worn at the beginning. She still looked classy, but she wasn't afraid to show what she had anymore.

Then there were those boots. Was it weird that seeing her in them made him hard? Like, every day?

The song ended and she seemed to come out of her thrall, glancing over at him like she was remembering he was there.

"Your friends are coming tomorrow night, right?" he asked.

"Yes, Cheryl, her fiancé, and another couple. I can't wait to see them, but I'm pretty nervous about performing in front of them."

She pulled off the highway, following the voice commands of the GPS. The streetlights came on as they headed through downtown Flagstaff and into the suburbs.

"You should have seen me the first time my parents came to one of my gigs. I wanted so bad for them to be proud."

"So what happened? Did you mess up?"

"Naw. I'd been playing those songs so long by then, I could have done them in my sleep. Your body remembers what to do. Even your voice does. You just need to trust it."

"I think I get what you mean. I think that's what happened the first night I performed. But I still don't trust myself completely. My strategy's always been to work at things until there's no possibility of failure."

"I guess that's one way to do it," he said.

"Maybe, but it's exhausting." She pulled up in front of a blue ranch house, the windows lit up and welcoming. "This must be it."

They were staying the next two nights with friends of Stu's, a professional couple in their forties who'd offered their guest bedroom and finished basement to the band. Beth was taking the extra bedroom.

The car ticked as the engine cooled and the car held them close in the quiet night. It was so similar to the way he used to pull up in front of a girl's house after a date when he was younger, that dark anticipation when the intimacy of the car pulled them together. Because when a girl lingered in the car and looked at him with soft eyes, she wanted to be kissed.

"This was a pretty great day, wasn't it?" Beth asked, her voice not much more than a whisper.

He could have told her that every day he spent with her was a great day, better than it could have been without her in it. But that was off limits, so he just smiled. "Yeah, it was."

Beth sighed, a flutter of sound and air that chased over his skin. Then the front door opened and a man and woman came out onto to the steps, ready to greet them.

Sometimes the girl wanted it but wasn't ready. And sometimes her dad opened the door and spoiled everything. Beth hadn't been waiting for a kiss, not really, but she was as reluctant to leave their little world as he was.

Sean and Myra had dinner ready, and the four of them sat down for the first home-cooked meal he'd had since he'd last visited his parents in May. Afterward he and Beth showered in the giant bathroom. He let Beth go first, hoping he might catch her walking by in nothing but a towel. Instead he had to content himself with the moist heat of the bathroom after she'd gone and her damp footprints on the bath mat.

The rest of the band showed up soon after and they all sat around drinking good wine and whisky and entertaining their hosts late into the night with stories from the road.

Myra and Sean called it a night first, Beth following on their heels. He and the rest of the guys headed into the basement and called dibs on the pull-out couch and air mattresses. There was a TV down there and they found a movie to watch, falling asleep one by one. Jesse turned the TV off and opened up his notebook. He had a new song in mind, one Beth could never hear. It started with a woman asleep behind a door he'd never enter.

***

"We're here!" Cheryl sang into the phone, the others calling out hello in the background.

Beth raced outside the club to find the four of them waiting on the sidewalk out front. Cheryl flew at her and then they were laughing and hugging like they'd been parted for years.

"How was the drive?" Beth asked.

"Jason was all manly and wouldn't let anyone else take over, so it was easy."

"Let me see that ring of yours," Beth said, grabbing Cheryl's left hand and holding it up so the sun lit the diamond, fracturing it into countless points of light.

"It's perfect." She turned to Jason, who stood smiling just behind Cheryl. "Congratulations on being a very smart man," she said, throwing her arms around him in a fierce hug.

Jason was blushing when she pulled back, and it was so adorable she almost couldn't stand it.

"She's missed you," he said, his eyes going straight to Cheryl. The two of them locked gazes and beamed at one another like no one else was in the room.

"They've been like that all week," Emily said, coming over to give Beth a hug. "You get used to it."

Cutter smiled and bent down to whisper something in Emily's ear. Emily made a face at him. "I did not," she whispered, laughing.

Beth had only met Cutter once before, but he gave her a warm smile and a kiss on the cheek.

"Thanks for the tickets," he said. "I can't even remember the last time I went to a show. I think I must be getting old."

"Aren't we all," Jason laughed.

"Not tonight we aren't," Cheryl declared. "Tonight we party."

"Are you guys hungry?" Beth asked. "I saw a couple places down the block that look good."

She'd already set up the merch table and rehearsed "Down by the River" with the band, so she had over an hour before she had to be back.

"We're all pretty hungry," Cheryl said, grabbing Beth's arm as they headed down the street.

They picked a Chinese restaurant that looked good. Even before they'd ordered they were peppering her with questions. Cheryl and Emily wanted to know what it was like working with Jesse, whether she missed Ohio, what it felt like to be onstage. Jason and Cutter said less and were more interested in logistics, like whether they were recording the shows and how the tour was funded.

Beth answered as much as she could without going into her feelings for Jesse, and eventually she managed to move the conversation away from herself. By the time they got back to the club a line had started at the doors, so she led them in through a side entrance and into the main room. A long bar ran down one side and tables were scattered along the walls. The floor in front of the stage was clear so people could crowd in front.

"I'd better get going," she said after they'd settled at a table. "You guys have fun and I'll come and get you after the show and bring you back to meet everyone."

Cheryl gave her another hug and Beth headed backstage, a huge smile stuck to her face. As weird as it felt to have her worlds collide, it was also wonderful. Besides, tonight wasn't just about her. She was only singing two songs. They were going to see Jesse live, and that was an experience she thought everyone should have before they died.

Backstage she checked in with Jesse to make sure she knew when she'd be singing, then found Stu to check if he needed her for anything.

"I don't want you back out here after you sing tonight," he said. "I'll take over when you go up, and you can wait backstage until the end of the show."

Her stomach turned over. "What? Why?"

"It doesn't make sense for people to see the woman performing with Jesse selling them t-shirts."

"Maybe I should stop singing then. I mean you hired me to–"

"Forget it. You two sound good up there. Besides, Jesse would go ballistic."

"But you hate the merch table."

"It's only for another week. Besides, you're still in charge of inventory, set-up, and counting it up at the end of the night."

Obviously it didn't make sense to argue anymore, and she could see his point. In any case, she still had work to do. She headed toward the green room, peeking over her shoulder one last time to see her friends. They were at the bar ordering drinks, all four smiling, clearly enjoying themselves.

She was installed at the table when the opening act went on. She had a great spot with a clear view to the stage, and she was closer than she usually was, which meant Jesse would be able to find her easily. She didn't like admitting even to herself how those looks he sent her while he played made her feel. But it was all part of the high she felt during the shows, part of the connection they had.

She made a bunch of sales, but the crowd evaporated when the band came on and launched into their first song. It was a good crowd tonight, exuberant but polite. Jesse liked rowdy crowds though, so he worked them up until they were yelling and whistling for more. By the third song Cheryl and her friends were out of their seats and in the middle of a writhing mass of bodies, their eyes fixed on the stage.

When they played the song right before she went on she quietly sang some scales and tried to empty her mind of everything but what she was singing. Usually she hated making her way through the crowd, knowing so many pairs of eyes were on her, but tonight she was too busy looking for Cheryl and laughing at the way her friend whistled and cat-called. As usual, Jesse treated her like she was some honored guest, meeting her at the stairs to take her hand.

As soon as she was up there with him everything else melted away and it was just the two of them, their voices blending into one. They sang the new song first, and after only a few bars the whole crowd was clapping along, shouting their approval. Before long she was feeling so loose and sure of herself she started to dance, and then before she knew what was happening Jesse had taken her hand and twirled her around until she was right next to him, singing into his microphone.

She was conscious of the audience's roar of approval as she looked out into the sea of rapt faces, and then she found Cheryl, Jason, Cutter and Emily, all of them smiling and dancing like they were having the time of their lives.

Jesse was giving it his all, paying for it with the blood that dripped off his knuckles and the sweat running down his cheeks. It pulled something out of her she wouldn't have known she had. She held nothing back, she'd learned that from him, and whereas in another life putting herself on the line would have been terrifying, nothing had ever felt better.

The crowd was going wild but settled down when the mellower notes of "Better Off" started. She'd sung the love song many times now, but something was different tonight. She stood there singing to Jesse, but this time she wasn't just delivering the song. She realized as she stood there inches from him, still singing into his mic, sharing his breath, his air, that she meant every word of the lyrics he'd written. It had become her truth.

She was in love with him.

The knowledge washed over her like a wave of pure sound. She shut her eyes for a moment, but there was no stopping it. It flowed through her with the music and the warmth of the lights, the warmth she saw in Jesse's smile when she opened her eyes again.

So she let it come, too wide open to fight it there on the stage in front of everyone. But she felt tears prick the back of her eyes when the song ended and he kissed her hand, sending her away.

She walked off stage and straight to the bathroom where she stared at herself in the mirror, dumbstruck. She loved him. She loved Jesse Rhodes, a man who could never be hers, would always be everyone else's. It was crazy and it was one-sided, but it was real.

She leaned against the sink, wrung out, not just from the revelation, but from the energy expended on stage. How Jesse played an entire show every night without flagging was a mystery. But it was that energy of his, a current that ran deep and strong, that pulled her in. Pulled her under.

So it was fine, she could handle this. As long as Jesse never found out.

She was backstage by the time they finished their encore and the lights came up, the band filing past her. Everything looked just a little different, like the world had tilted one degree on its axis. Even her body felt lighter, less substantial.

"Nice job, guys" she said, trying to be normal, to ground herself in the usual things.

Jesse was the last one off stage, and his attention was all on her despite people shouting his name from the other side of the curtain.

"That was amazing," he said, pulling her toward him. "Something happened out there. Did you feel it?"

She could feel how amped he was. You could have powered the whole city off the energy radiating from him. What would it be like to have all that energy pouring into her?

She smiled. "Yeah, I felt it." She pulled her hand away from his, stepping back. "I'd better go grab my friends."

"Oh, right. You're going to bring them backstage, right?"

"If that's okay."

"Of course. I want to meet them."

The four of them were standing together, their excitement palpable. As soon as Cheryl spotted her she ran at Beth with a shriek, nearly knocking her over as she threw her arms around her.

"Oh my God. That was incredible. You were amazing. Wasn't she amazing?" Cheryl asked, turning to the others. "I couldn't even believe it," she went on before anyone could say a word. "I almost peed my pants when you started to sing."

Beth could only laugh at Cheryl's exuberance. "I'm glad you liked it."

"I didn't just *like* it. I'm trying to tell you something here. I was floored. All this time you've been living this quiet life, and you had this...this inner rock goddess in you."

"I think that might be a slight exaggeration. I mean, I did all right, but Jesse would make anyone look good."

Cheryl squeezed her arm, her expression mutinous. "The hell with that. *You* make *him* look good."

"She's right," Jason said. "You were spectacular. It's a whole other side of you I didn't know about. But then, I haven't known you for long."

"Well I have, and I didn't know it was there, either." Cheryl was looking at Beth with narrowed eyes, assessing her.

Did she see something different?

Emily grabbed her in a fierce hug. "Not everyone can do what you do," she said. She spoke low, just for Beth. "Whatever it means to you, just make sure you don't undervalue it."

She wasn't sure what to say to that. Emily had been a professional ballet dancer and she was a tough critic. She didn't give praise lightly, which made her comment all the more striking.

"The show rocked," Cutter said. "No wonder I'm suddenly hearing him all over the place. That guy's going places."

There was that bittersweet pang she'd been feeling this past week, only now it was more of an ache. But she wasn't going to think about all that now. Maybe there wasn't even much to think about. Her feelings had grown and changed, but nothing else needed to change. She'd enjoy herself and finish out the tour, and she'd appreciate every moment of it.

Right now, she was going to enjoy the fact that her friends were in town and she was going to show them a good time. They helped her pack up the table and Jason and Cutter insisted on carrying all the boxes, so she was finished in no time. The routine tasks helped bring her back into herself, and by the time they were done, she no longer felt in danger of being blown into the ether.

Both bands, along with a bunch of their friends and people she didn't know, were already deep into party mode in the green room. As usual Jesse was surrounded by half a dozen people, but the second Beth and her friends entered the room he came over to greet them. Beth made the introductions, her heart picking up speed. She needed her friends to like him, to see some of what she saw.

"This is Cheryl, Jason, Emily and Cutter."

Jesse shook hands all around, then turned back to Cheryl. "So you've known Beth since she was a little girl, huh? What did you think of her tonight?"

"I thought she was perfect, and you're lucky to have gotten her so cheap."

Jesse threw back his head and laughed. "Right on both counts," he said, looking at Beth with a little smile.

"We'll discuss payment later," Beth said. "Let's get these guys a drink."

Cutter, Jason and Jesse got talking about places they'd all been, and before long they were so involved, they barely noticed when Emily, Cheryl and Beth moved away.

The second they were out of earshot Emily turned to Beth. "You have some serious willpower. If I was traveling with that man, I'm not sure I'd have the strength of character you have."

"It wasn't quite so hard at first, not when I saw women throwing themselves at him. He could sleep with a different woman every night if he wanted."

"Does he?" Cheryl asked.

"Not lately, I don't think. He slept with someone the first night I was on tour, but I haven't seen him with anyone else. He's kind of made a point of telling me he hasn't, but we're not sleeping together, so there's no reason for him not to."

"That man looks at you like you mean something," Cheryl said.

"What are you talking about?"

Cheryl rolled her eyes and looked at Emily, as if for help. "Am I wrong about this?"

"No. If I had to bet money, I'd say he's nuts about her."

Beth's heart slammed into her chest, but she didn't let on. What did they know, anyway? They were just suffering the effects of Jesse's mortal hotness. She couldn't let herself fall into some silly fantasy. It was one thing to acknowledge her love for him. It was another to believe he returned it.

"Guys, you've seen us together for like, five minutes."

"We also saw you together on stage. Now I understand what all the buzz is about on Twitter."

"Oh my God," Beth groaned. "You do not read all that stuff."

"How else am I supposed to know what's going on with you?" Cheryl said. "You barely call anymore."

"We're getting off topic here," Emily interjected. "I agree that Jesse has the hots for you. Maybe more than the hots. He watches you when you're not looking."

"He does?"

"He does," Cheryl said with a firm nod. "That man is yearning."

"That's...interesting," Beth said, wishing she were near a chair. "I mean I know he has the hots for me. He hasn't been shy about that. And obviously we like each other. We have a great time together..." It was on the tip of her tongue to tell them she loved him, but she couldn't, not in the middle of so many people. "It doesn't matter," she said, shaking her head to clear it. "Getting involved with Jesse isn't part of the plan."

"What plan is that?" Emily asked.

"To find a man I can trust and a life that *I* choose."

"That's a good plan," Emily said, her hand on Beth's arm. "Just because a man wants you doesn't mean he gets to have you."

"Agreed," Cheryl said. "I just want you to be happy, and you seem happier than I've ever seen you. You're... radiant. I mean, you were always gorgeous, but it's like you've stopped hiding your light under a rock." She tipped her head and looked at Beth with a whimsical smile. "Whatever it is that's making you so happy, I want you to have it."

Tears sprung to Beth's eyes without warning. "That's the nicest thing anyone's ever said to me," she said, bending down to give her friend a fierce hug.

Then Emily was hugging her too and the three of them were laughing and hugging, nearly falling over in the process.

"Wow, are they drunk already?"

It was Jason, with Cutter and Jesse right behind him.

"Could you take a picture of us, babe?" Cheryl asked, handing Jason her phone.

Beth stood with an arm around Emily and Cheryl and smiled for the camera. "Now one with all of you and Jesse," she ordered. "Someday he'll be a big rock star and you'll get to show this to your children."

"What do you mean, *someday*?" Jesse asked, mock offended.

Beth took the photo, conscious the whole time of Jesse's warm gaze on her. Was that the look Emily and Cheryl were talking about?

"Now one with just me and Beth," Jesse said, pulling her close.

Beth smiled and put her arm around his waist, praying she wasn't completely transparent. Even being in a crowd of people didn't stop the awareness that flooded through her.

It was easier to keep her expectations at bay if she thought his interest in her was purely sexual. But what if it was more than that for him? Did that even matter? It didn't change the fact that in a week he'd be gone from her life completely.

Until now she'd thought of Jesse only as a bad choice, maybe even a dangerous one. But there was no denying that she was happy around him, happier than she remembered being with anyone else. What a strange twist of fate to be happiest around someone who could only make her miserable.

Cheryl took the picture, but Jesse's arm stayed right where it was.

"Do you mind if I steal Beth for a minute?" he asked. "I want to introduce her to a few folks."

Cheryl and Emily exchanged meaningful looks.

"Of course not," Cheryl said.

"Help yourself to another drink," Jesse told them, his arm slipping from Beth's shoulders so he could grab her hand. "I'll bring her right back."

It was only as she walked away with her hand in Jesse's that she realized none of this was out of the ordinary. He always threw his arm around her or touched her in some way. He smiled and joked with her, introduced her to his friends. She'd just gotten so used to it she hadn't thought much about what it looked like to other people.

She was still thinking about everything Cheryl and Emily had said a little later when she circled back to where her friends sat on one of the couches. Cheryl was perched on Jason's lap, her head tucked into his neck, and Emily leaned drunkenly against Cutter and gave a delicate yawn.

"You guys look beat," Beth said, smiling down at them.

"It's after two. We can't all be rock stars," Cheryl mumbled.

"Excuse me? You two were strippers. Are you telling me you can't outlast me now?"

"'Were' being the operative word," Jason said. "This one's in bed by ten every night."

"You've officially out-paced us," Emily pronounced. She sat up and stretched her arms over her head, even that simple gesture graceful. "I'd better get some sleep, too. I teach class tomorrow afternoon. You can't be sleep-deprived around ten-year-olds."

Jason scooped Cheryl up and set her on her feet as he stood. Cutter steadied Emily when she stumbled against him. The four of them were a study in full-hearted, committed love, and her chest squeezed once in painful recognition that whatever Jesse felt for her, it wasn't this.

She walked them out to Jason's car. "You know how to get to the hotel?"

"Yeah, we're good," Cutter said, opening the car door for Emily. "It's just down the street."

"I'm so glad you guys made it."

Cheryl threw her arms around Beth. "Are you kidding? We wouldn't have missed it for anything."

Then they were talking at once, laughing and saying goodnight.

"See you in a week!" Cheryl yelled out the window, and she didn't stop waving until the car was out of sight.

"Your friends have a good time?" Jesse asked when she got back to the party.

"Yeah. They think you're pretty great. Of course, they think I'm greater." She laughed. "Cheryl's never seen me do anything like that. I've always been pretty quiet."

"Quiet's good, but you shouldn't hide away, either."

"I'm not sure I could anymore," she said, the realization hitting her all at once. She wasn't sure how she felt about it, though. "I'm pretty beat," she said, pushing away from the wall before he could say anything. "I think I'll head back to the house. I'll see you in the morning?"

"Well, more like the afternoon." He was smiling again, though he looked more subdued.

"Right, silly me. Get some sleep. You're driving tomorrow," she said, heading for the door.

Because she absolutely could not stand looking into his eyes one more second.

Chapter Ten

What's it like to be the only woman in the band, Beth?"

Beth looked up from her laptop, eyes wary. "Aren't you supposed to be interviewing Jesse?"

"I think our readers would be interested in hearing from you as well," the reporter, a woman named Jean Thomas, replied.

Jesse didn't jump in right away. As surprised as he was by the woman's question, he wasn't bothered by it. Beth had been performing on stage for a while now, and it was natural people would be asking questions. But if Beth didn't want to answer them, that was another thing.

"I'm not part of the band," Beth said. "I sing a couple of songs, that's all."

He could tell she was trying not to seem rude or impatient, but she was obviously anxious to be left alone.

They were sitting in a coffee shop near the club in Fort Worth for a pre-show print interview. Beth only went along on interviews in order to jump in if a reporter got too invasive. Stu thought it was better to have someone else tell a reporter to back off, and Jesse had learned the hard way that Stu was right. If you pissed off a reporter, you'd sure as hell see it in their write-up.

Beth always sat nearby and worked with one ear tuned to the interview. There'd been a couple of occasions when she'd jumped in after a reporter had asked about women or drugs on the road, but that had been the extent of her involvement.

"Maybe you're not officially in the band," the reporter pushed on, "but you've been traveling with them for weeks now. There's speculation that the two of you are an item. Care to comment?"

"We sing a couple of songs together," Beth said, her tone civil but not much more. "It's nothing more than that."

"You have great chemistry on stage. Fans are curious about whether that extends backstage, too."

A flush was spreading up her neck and coloring her cheeks. She looked...embarrassed, angry? He wasn't sure, but it was clear enough she was unhappy.

"Beth started singing as a favor to me," he said, hoping to turn the attention away from her. "I wanted to work on some songs before I went into the studio."

"The audience seems to love her. Anything thoughts of keeping her on?"

He hadn't expected that.

"Well, no. She's got other things she wants to do. This was more of a time-out for her."

The reporter was taking this all down in some sort of shorthand Jesse couldn't decipher.

"Ah, so the two of you will be parting soon, is that it?"

Jesse stood up. "I think we're finished here," he said, doing his best to tamp down his anger.

"Wait, I was just–"

But Jesse was done. It was bad enough he had to sit through these things. He wasn't going to put Beth through it, too.

Beth closed her laptop and stood up. "You can email either myself or Stu MIrsky if you have any further questions," Beth said. She slung her laptop over her shoulder. "Enjoy the show."

"Well, that was fun," Jesse said once they were out on the sidewalk.

Beth smiled briefly but didn't say anything. She'd been quiet all day. In fact, she'd been oddly quiet the last few days. Nothing he could put his finger on, really. Just a little quieter, more withdrawn. Less *there*. The connection he'd felt with her was evaporating and he didn't know what to do about it. The only time he felt it now was onstage.

Was she tired of the tour, tired of him? He couldn't tell and was afraid to ask. All he knew was he was losing her even sooner than he'd expected, and he'd never really had her in the first place.

They split up back at the club. She no longer needed to rehearse her two songs, so she took care of all her usual tasks while they ran through soundcheck. He caught up with her afterwards as she finished setting up the merch table.

"Want to try that Thai place we saw near the coffee shop?" he asked.

"You guys go ahead. I have some stuff I want to take care of."

"Oh, okay. We'll catch up with you later then," he said, trying not to show how his heart sank.

He drank a little more than usual in an effort to take his mind off Beth, but his frustration was still simmering when he went on. As usual he looked for her, but seeing her tonight didn't ground him like it usually did. Instead he felt like an open circuit, all his energy rushing out into nothing.

He was in the middle of a song when he glanced her way again and saw her trying to shake off some guy. Keeping his eyes on them as he played, he watched her shake her head, frowning as she took a step back. The guy lurched toward her, obviously drunk, and grabbed her arm.

She was struggling now, trying to pull away without any success, her expression something between fear and disgust.

Jesse stopped playing.

"Hey, take your hands off her, motherfucker," he yelled, walking to the edge of the stage.

The crowd fell silent as the band came to a ragged stop behind him.

"Fuck you, asshole," the guy yelled back, his hand still on Beth's arm.

Jesse jumped off the stage and into the crowd. People drew back, but he saw only Beth as he made his way to her. The guy who'd grabbed her was about his own height and weight, but he didn't seem to be expecting his right hook.

The guy stumbled and went down like a sack of potatoes. Jesse stood over him, his heartbeat pounding in his ears, and waited to see if he'd get up. He kind of hoped he would because he really wanted to pound on something. But the guy just blinked up at him, as if unsure why he was on the floor, and then the bouncers finally arrived and dragged him away.

Beth was staring at him like he'd lost his mind.

"You okay?" he asked her, his breathing fast and heavy.

"You're crazy," she said, giving him a push on the shoulder. "Get back up there and finish your show."

"Answer me first."

"Yes, I'm fine. Don't worry about me."

He hesitated, but the entire room was looking at them, and the buzz of conversation had risen to a roar.

"Dude, that was awesome," he heard someone say as he made his way back to the stage.

Matt was staring at him, either impressed or appalled, he couldn't tell which. "Holy shit, Jesse. That was insane."

He picked up his guitar and turned back to the crowd. "What do you say we take that last one from the top?" he said, all easy-like.

As if he weren't still high on adrenaline. Not to mention rage, lust, and every other damn thing.

His voice and playing were as raw as his nerves the rest of the set. Whenever he looked over at Beth her eyes were on him, her expression one he'd never seen before. He couldn't tell if it was one of pleasure or misery.

"I can't fucking believe you did that," Stu spat, storming toward him the second he came off stage for intermission. "What if you'd broken your hand?"

"My hand's fine," Jesse said, ignoring the throbbing in his knuckles. He *was* lucky he hadn't broken anything. "What was I supposed to do? Stand there and watch some guy maul her? Anyway, people think it was cool."

"Fuck cool. That guy could sue us. They have bouncers to deal with that shit, you know."

"They took too long."

Stu stared at him, his eyes bulging out of his head. "This isn't one of those dives you used to play with Buddy's band. This is a nice place, Jesse. We can't afford for you to get a reputation now."

"Just let it go, Stu."

A vein throbbed in Stu's forehead. Never a good sign.

"You want me to let it go? Ask the fucking internet to let it go. Someone's already posted video of you beating up one of your own fans."

Hmm. he hadn't thought of that. That wasn't great.

"Okay, I admit that's not ideal, but it's over and done with. Besides, this is rock 'n roll. People have done a lot worse."

More glaring from Stu.

"Can we talk about this later? I need a drink."

Stu's nostrils flared and he took a couple of deep breaths before turning and stalking away.

The guys looked up as he entered the back room.

"I can't believe I'm saying this, but maybe you should just sleep with her," Matt said. "It'd be better than beating people up."

Jesse drank an entire bottle of water and collapsed onto one of the couches. Still he said nothing, because he and Beth were not open for discussion. Though he couldn't agree more. Then again, he'd have punched the guy even if he were sleeping with Beth.

And even after that whole scene, she was still out there, selling their shit. What if some other asshole bothered her?

He grabbed a beer to settle his nerves and noodled around on his guitar, picking out the new song he'd been working on. Another duet, this one about wanting someone you couldn't have. There was no hiding the inspiration behind "In Another Life," which meant he couldn't ask Beth to sing it with him. But even as he wrote it he imagined her voice, imagined her sitting beside him as they tried different arrangements.

If he couldn't have her, couldn't he at least have that?

***

People came to the table during intermission and looked at her with wide-eyed curiosity. A few asked if she was all right. No one seemed to think badly of Jesse, thank goodness. As to what she thought...she was still stunned by the sight of him charging through the crowd in her defense. She'd never seen him that angry, never seen him violent, though apparently he'd gone after Will that day in Missoula.

He shouldn't have punched the guy. It had been unnecessary and not great PR, but worse than that was the way it shattered the calm shell she'd been trying to create. She'd taken a step back, just enough to give her distance and allow her some self-preservation. But Jesse kept breaking through and making her feel too much.

The shows were another thing. Up on stage she didn't hide anything. There was no room for it, and it felt too good to give herself over to his songs.

Jesse was always changing the set list, and tonight he called her up more than halfway through the second set. The crowd was ecstatic, their hair wet with sweat, bodies swaying, voices hoarse from hollering their approval. The knowledge that the night was almost over seemed to fuel them to even greater heights.

Beth was ready to join in again, to step into all that heat and energy, burn off the need she'd felt ever since Jesse came storming over and laid that guy flat out for her.

Once she was on stage she wanted it to go on forever, wanted to wrap herself in the music and let it keep her in that perfect spot, that perfect feeling. Next to Jesse, where they could take what they had together to the highest point possible, experience everything in those songs it was possible to feel. The way they couldn't offstage.

But her part in his life was small, as was her part in each show. After the second song she walked off and went backstage. Tonight she wasn't up to watching him from the wings. Instead she made her way to a storage area in the back and called her mother.

"Beth, honey."

"Hi, Mom."

"Did you get my message? Are you coming home for Thanksgiving?"

"Of course I'll be there. I'm always there."

"I just wanted to be sure. How are things? Any luck with the job hunt?"

As usual she cringed at having to lie to her mother. At least that wouldn't last much longer.

"Not yet, but I've got enough savings to tide me over. I'm thinking about trying something a bit different."

"Like what?"

"It's another area of accounting," she said. She didn't really feel like explaining what a business manager for artists was. "But I think it'd be interesting. I just need to find out the best way to get into it."

Her mother sounded relieved that she wasn't making a big change. She and her father always advised caution, the need to think things through and not act spontaneously. That's when you made mistakes, did things you later regretted.

They spent the rest of the conversation talking about people Beth knew in Gulliver. By the time she got off the phone the audience was clapping for an encore.

Just one more gig in Austin and it was over. Maybe it was stupid to be trying to avoid the pain that was coming her way. Soon she wouldn't have any of it. Even so she stayed hidden in the bathroom and listened to the band come off stage and head down to the green room. She stayed there until the whole building had quieted, and when she finally emerged she found Stu making sales to a few last customers.

Stu looked up, obviously relieved to see her. By the time they finished tallying sales and packing everything up the only people left were them and the staff sweeping the floors.

"Everyone's gone to the bar down the block," Stu said. "You going?"

"Probably not," she said. "But you go ahead, I can finish up here."

Stu started to protest but she waved him off. "If you take care of those," she said, gesturing to a couple of cartons, "I can handle the rest."

Stu acquiesced and headed out to the van with his arms full.

It didn't take her long to finish up, but she still wasn't sure whether she was up to going to the bar. Her head wasn't in the right space for partying, but neither did she want to head back to the hotel. She was far too restless to call it a night, and too scared to do what she really wanted.

She'd just put the last two boxes in the car and closed the door when she heard the scuff of feet on concrete.

She turned around to find Jesse, looking pissed. He was in a fresh t-shirt and had obviously cleaned up, but he looked no more civilized for it.

"What the hell are you doing out here all alone?"

"What are you talking about?"

"It's after midnight and you're alone in a goddamn parking lot. What the hell was Stu thinking?"

"I'm fine, Jesse. You don't need to worry about me."

He was keyed up, probably from the fight as much as from the show. She could see it in the set of his shoulders. Usually he was all loose cowboy, but at the moment he looked dangerous.

"You have no idea who might have given you trouble out here."

They were all alone, it was late, and the way he was looking at her stirred up every feeling she'd been trying so hard to bury. Whatever was running through Jesse was running through her too, and it made her careless. Or maybe she was just done being careful.

"Right now I just see you."

He stared at her for several long seconds, his chest heaving. Then he came toward her. She backed up as he pressed in, her breath catching as she bumped up against the car. He braced a hand on either side of her head and stared at her, his eyes dropping to her lips.

"Don't push me, honey." His voice was tense, stripped raw from singing and tight with need. "I've had about as much as I can take."

She watched him want her, felt him grow hard against her belly. Sweat broke out across her breasts and neck, her lower back. She was shaking. Maybe it was from holding herself back, or for not knowing how to ask for what she wanted.

She closed her eyes for several long moments, desire warring with the doubt she'd grown so accustomed to. She couldn't do this, but she couldn't turn away, either. Every day she'd been on tour with him, every note they'd sung together had been leading to this. Maybe it was time she stopped running from it.

She tipped her hips into his and cupped his face in her palms, heard his breath catch as she took his mouth.

God, his mouth. It was sin itself. She brushed her lips over his, loving the scrape of his jaw against her smoother skin. She licked into him, finding her way hesitantly at first, but the groan that tore from him made her bolder. In moments she was stroking deep, tasting him, hungry for everything he had.

A shudder ran through his body, and then his hands were on her ass as he stepped between her thighs. She was wearing a skirt tonight, thank the sweet lord, and he slid it higher so that his jeans rubbed the tender skin of her inner thighs. He rolled into her, letting her feel how much he wanted her, and she was instantly so wet he could have had her then and there.

He took over, took the kiss deeper, slower, tasting and withdrawing in a rhythm so carnal she arched against him and moaned. His mouth moved down her throat, licked at the hollow before dropping down to close over a tight peak.

Pushing his t-shirt up she dragged her nails lightly back down. In answer his hand sank into her hips and he thrust into her. Again and again he moved against her, the movement so sexual and yet so far from actual sex she wanted to scream.

"Please, Jesse," she begged him, writhing against him.

"That's right, honey," he rasped, his mouth back at her ear. He still held her with his hips, but he'd stopped moving. "Beg me for it. Show me how much you want it."

She bit his shoulder, dug her fingers into his ass.

His laugh was dark and pleased as he pulled away, the night air cool on her heated skin. She started to protest only to be stopped breathless by his hand skimming over her thigh, pushing her skirt back up.

"You need something?" he whispered, his fingers finding the soaking wet placket of her underwear. He groaned as she bucked against his hand and he slid over her slow and then a little faster. She would have given anything for him to touch her without any barriers between them.

"More, Jesse."

Her hands were fisted in his shirt and she couldn't take her eyes off the look on his face as he watched his own hand slide over her. She held her breath as he moved higher and slipped inside. His breath hissed as he stroked over her swollen folds, finding her clit with a calloused fingertip.

"You want me to make you come, honey?" he whispered, his finger stroking, stroking, paying attention to her sounds and adjusting to what she liked.

"Yes, God, yes."

"I want that, too. I've wanted that forever."

She was getting close, the circle of pleasure getting tighter, more focused.

The slam of a door jolted her out of her spiral. Jesse pulled his hand away and turned around, shielding her from view. They watched as the club's manager came out the back door and walked to his car on the other side of the lot.

Jesse turned around and looked at her. "I'm taking you back to the hotel."

"But what about Stu and –"

"Are you trying to kill me?" he asked her.

"I'll drive," she said, opening the driver's side door. "I know for a fact there's no more blood left in your brain."

He slid into the car and she pulled out of the lot, grateful she had the steering wheel to grip. She risked a look at him, but he was staring out the side window. She reached out and put a hand on his thigh and he jumped an inch off the seat.

"Sorry, I just thought..."

"The second we're inside that room I want you naked. Can you do that for me?"

She squirmed on the seat, the need in his voice enough to hollow her out. They were silent the last couple of miles to her hotel. Everyone else was staying with friends spread around town, so no one would know anything except that Jesse had left the bar early. Maybe they'd think he went out with friends or home with another woman. Maybe they'd know it was her.

She no longer cared.

Chapter Eleven

Jesse followed Beth into the room and closed the door. He could hear her unsteady breathing as she moved across the room and turned on a standing lamp in the far corner.

He took a deep breath himself, tamping down the rough urgency from the parking lot. Now that he knew he had her, he could take his time. This was Beth. He needed to make it good for her.

She came back toward him, her hands clasped in front of her like she didn't know what to do with them. Light from the far away lamp fell across her face and she looked down, suddenly shy. It was that mix of shyness and boldness that made her so appealing, so unlike any woman he'd known.

"So I should just take all my clothes off?" she said, toeing off one red boot, then the other.

Just the sight of her taking off her boots nearly killed him.

"I changed my mind," he said, closing the distance between them. "If I see all of you right now this won't last nearly as long as I want it to."

"Oh, okay," she said, looking relieved and a little pleased she was driving him so crazy.

A horniness so profound he thought it might kill him swept over him then. He closed his eyes and breathed through it. When he opened them she was smiling, and it was the same beam of light she turned on him in the car, the same one she gave him on stage when she sang a sassy lyric.

He kissed her again, because goddamn he could kiss this woman all night, and they sure as hell hadn't done enough of it. She was ready for it, groaning into his mouth as his lips closed over hers and wrapping her arms around his neck. He kept himself in check and let her explore, his whole body hardening when her tongue slipped into his, tentative at first and then demanding.

Within seconds they were at full heat, pressed together against their entire length and trying to get closer. He'd never wanted anything more than Beth naked on that bed, but still he held back, determined to make it last.

Her hands slid under his t-shirt and up his back, nails lightly scratching. He pulled away and looked down at her heavy-lidded eyes and swollen mouth, at the damp strands of hair that stuck to her temples.

"Goddamn, you're gorgeous," he breathed, taking her mouth again.

Only this time it wasn't slow or patient. He wanted to take everything she had, make her as crazy as he was. She opened up and gave it to him, her hands sliding down to his hips and pulling him harder against her.

He needed her on her back, now. Grabbing her ass he pulled her up against him, her gasp going straight to his cock. He carried her to the bed and came down on top of her, settling between her spread thighs. She arched into him, baring her throat. He licked her there, wanting to feel the blood pounding through her in time with his own. He breathed her in, finding the scent he'd been chasing so long, her musk and soap, her sweat and need.

Bending down he took a tight nipple in his mouth through her t-shirt, sucking on her through his own name written across her chest. That's how he wanted her, branded by him, so everyone knew who she belonged to.

As desperate as he was to be inside her, he'd been desperate for this, too. So he took his time, sucking on each peak, rolling them around between his fingers as he watched her face. She liked it all, but she especially liked when he gently bit down at the same time.

Then she was pushing on his chest, asking him to back off. Panic speared through him that she wanted him to stop, but when she sat up, her eyes were burning, her cheeks flushed.

"Take this off," she demanded, grabbing the hem of his shirt and yanking it up.

He pulled it the rest of the way off. She was kneeling before him now, her hands and mouth all over him, kissing his neck, running over his chest and stomach. He held her by the waist, drunk on her, trying to hold it together. Then her hands went to his belt buckle and her head dipped and she licked his nipple.

He had her on her back again the next second.

"Wait, no," she protested. "I need to touch you."

"That can wait. This can't," he said, barely able to speak. He moved lower, cruising down her long body. Her skirt pooled around her waist, baring those thighs he'd been dreaming about for so long. Tension had made her muscles stand out strong and lean. Her pale blue underwear covered her, but just barely. They were so soaked through, they'd become nearly transparent.

Her whole body jerked and her hips came up, pressing harder into him as her thighs spread wider. He stayed there for a second, breathing her in, holding her down as he sucked her through the fabric. She was his now, so hot and ready she was drinking up whatever he gave her, every little movement calling forth a gasp or moan.

He lost his hold when she reared up, eyes blazing. Then she was pulling her shirt off and tearing off her bra. He watched in amazement as she stood up on the bed and slid her skirt and underwear off together, flinging them to the floor. He stared, mouth dry, at the sight of all that skin, the curves of her hips and thighs, her full breasts.

She looked down at him. "Take your clothes off this second or I swear to God I will lose it."

Well, that was pretty clear. He got off the bed, got naked, and pulled a condom out of his duffel bag. She was kneeling on the bed now, watching him.

"Put that on," she commanded.

He did. He was so turned on, even the feel of his own hand made him gasp.

Her eyes stayed fixed on him as he climbed back in, kissing her as he pressed her back down. She started to protest.

"What, you want to get on top?" he asked, just barely in control, so hungry for her he was a little afraid of himself.

She nodded and grabbed his cock.

He wasn't small, and he'd learned to go slow, but the way Beth was looking at him made him want to drive into her and ride her till he didn't know his own name.

"Later," he said, and entered her in one thrust.

She gasped and drew her knees up and dug her heels into his ass, urging him deeper. She was tight, tighter than he'd expected, but so wet there was no resistance. Fucking heaven. He withdrew and thrust again, and she bucked beneath him.

He looked away from where their bodies joined and watched her face as he pulled out and sank into her fully. God, she was beautiful. All the days and hours with her couldn't have prepared him for Beth like this.

He needed to get deeper, closer, under her skin, in her heart. She was lifting into him, the two of them surging together. She opened her eyes and looked at him, her eyes dazed under heavy lids. He felt every shiver and tremble with a kind of awe he'd never known.

Pulling back just a little he snuck his thumb between them and went straight to the hard pearl of her clit. He stroked her as he thrust deep and steady, a primitive pleasure surging through him as she arched into him, gasping his name as she shattered around him. She was still shaking with aftershocks when he drove into her, again and again, calling her name, his release so intense his vision went white.

***

One of Beth's hands rested on Jesse's fine, tight ass, the other on his shoulder. She lay there, boneless, absorbing the feel of him on top of her, his weight welcome after the way she'd flown apart moments ago.

With a low groan he lifted himself up on his forearms and looked down at her. "You all right, honey?"

She nodded, not quite able to speak, and gave him a shaky smile. "Just a little dazed. That was…"

"Yeah, it was."

Leaning down he kissed her, slow and soft, pulling away to look at her. His eyes were serious but a little smile curled the corner of his mouth. She gripped him tighter as he started to withdraw.

He gave little laugh and pulled away. "I'll be right back," he said, rolling off the bed and padding to the bathroom.

She was physically sated, her limbs heavy, the need that had been drumming through her for weeks finally quiet. But the love and doubt she'd been keeping at bay met no resistance as they rose to the surface. He'd just shattered all her barriers, all the ways she had of protecting herself. Had he been able to sense how she felt about him? What would he do if he knew? This was about sex for him, nothing more. Or maybe that wasn't fair. It was more than sex, but certainly less than love.

She was still lying naked on top of the covers, but her body was cooling, her worries speeding up, and she felt far too vulnerable exposed as she was. Pushing back the blankets she climbed underneath, pulling them up to her chest.

The toilet flushed and water ran. Her heart rate, which had been slowing down, jump-started at the sight of Jesse coming out and heading toward her. He was too much– too much man, too much heat and light. How was she supposed to survive him now?

"You cold?" he asked, climbing in beside her. "I can turn the air off."

"I'm okay," she said, turning toward him.

Because even now, *especially* now, she couldn't do otherwise.

"Tell me I can stay the night," he coaxed, his voice a rough whisper in her ear.

"You'd better," she said, her arms coming around him, drawing him close.

This was the way to survive Jesse. Lose herself in him without thought for what came next. Take what she wanted now and worry about what she'd be left with later. If there was anything she'd learned this past month, it was that.

"If I'd known this was in store for us, I wouldn't have given a shit about the band or the tour," Jesse said, his hand stroking her from thigh to hip, then up her arm to her shoulder. "I'd have been on you from day one."

She tried to imagine what that would have been like. "I think I needed to work up to this. I probably would have had a heart attack if you'd come at me, guns blazing, right from the start."

He laughed, but his expression turned thoughtful. "It wouldn't have been this good at the start, either. It's not just sex anymore."

He flushed and looked away, as if surprised by his own admission, and a little flare of hope went up in her chest. Then he was kissing her again, working his way down her throat to her breasts where he lingered, rolling and sucking her nipples like he had all the time in the world to drive her crazy.

She had the brief thought that he was trying to distract her with sex, or trying to avoid an uncomfortable topic, but soon she couldn't think about much besides what he was doing to her.

"You're even more gorgeous than I thought you'd be," he murmured, the ends of his hair brushing over her skin.

"Come here, let me touch you."

"Not yet, honey. I've still got some bases to cover." He moved lower, sliding down the bed until he was between her legs. "Now this, this is dessert," he said, dipping his head.

Her hips rose to meet him, thighs falling open as he licked into her, light and teasing at first, waking her up again. Her need turned dark and urgent fast, and soon she was impatient, greedy for more.

Jesse hummed his approval, slowing as if to savor the taste of her. She could smell their sex and her own sweat as she grew hot and needy. She'd never seen anything hotter than Jesse between her legs, and she pushed her fingers into his messy hair and urged him on.

He praised her, coaxed her, slid his tongue inside her like there was no place he wouldn't go, all the while holding her hips to the bed as she climbed toward her release. But she didn't want to go there alone. She wanted him inside her, filling the hollow that grew along with her pleasure.

Jesse protested as she slid out from under him. "You were so close."

"You're damn right I am, and I want you inside me."

She pulled another condom from his bag and ripped it open as she climbed back on the bed. He was hard and huge, more than ready. He moved to press her back but she shook her head.

"Oh no. You said later. This is later," she said, pushing him onto the mattress.

Another man might have looked passive, but not Jesse. He looked more like an animal biding its time before it struck.

She swung a leg over him and took him slowly, drawing it out, her swollen folds ultra sensitive.

"Sweet Jesus," he breathed, his hands on her hips.

But he didn't rush her, much as she felt him wanting to. They both gasped as she came to rest on him and her heart beat in her ears as they looked at each other. She stayed, there, poised between wanting and having, need and fulfillment.

Jesse cupped her face in his hands and pulled her down to him, his kiss deep and long and tasting faintly of her own excitement. His tongue stroked into her as he thrust, and she rose up and came down, again and again, slow and then faster. Jesse kept pace, his eyes fixed on her, his chest heaving. She could feel his need coiling in him but he held back and let her lead, matching her rhythm.

She was getting close again. She spread her thighs, took him deeper. Jesse grazed her clit with his thumb, then again.

"Yes, God yes. Do that."

He stopped teasing and stroked over her, hissing through his teeth as her head fell back and called his name.

***

Beth came out of the shower, a towel wrapped around her middle for modesty. Jesse was sitting up against the headboard dressed only in jeans, his hair still wet. His guitar was out, a notebook on his lap.

He grinned at her, eyes narrowing. "This reminds me of the day I saw you after you'd come out of the pool."

"I was wearing a swimsuit under my towel that day."

"You looked pretty naked to me." He strummed a few chords. "Why are you wearing that? Afraid I'll ravage you?"

She gave him what she hoped was a worldly sort of look, though she could feel herself blushing. "Maybe. I can barely walk as it is."

"Hey, that last one's on you, honey. Admit it, you're insatiable."

It was true. The sight of Jesse bare-chested on the bed was revving her up all over again, and they'd already had sex three times, the last time no more than an hour ago.

Something on her face must have given her away, because he went very still, homing in on her.

His voice was low, dark and reasonable and dangerous. "You know, you're gonna have to drop that towel sometime."

She was just starting to consider another go with him when the hotel room phone rang. They both stared at it like it was some unknown machine.

"That's weird. Who'd be calling me here?"

But as soon as she asked she knew the answer. She'd turned off her phone last night, but it was almost noon and Stu had probably been trying to reach her. She picked up on the third ring.

"Why the hell is your phone off?" Stu demanded.

"Sorry, I didn't realize. What's up?"

"I just booked another print interview for four o'clock, so you'll have to get moving."

"That's going to be tight. He's got two more right after that and the radio spot."

"I know, but this is Rolling Stone, so I wasn't about to say no."

"Wow, okay. We'll be out of here in a few minutes."

Jesse's eyebrows rose and too late she realized what she'd said.

Stu's voice took on a slight edge. "Jesse's with you in your hotel room?"

"Um, you could say that."

Silence, then one of Stu's patented weary sighs.

"Whatever, I don't need to know. Just do me a favor and don't rub Will's face in it. I'd like the band to get through the last show intact."

"Of course."

They went over a few other details and she hung up.

"Cat out of the bag?" Jesse asked.

"Yes, but he took it well enough. More importantly, you have an interview with Rolling Stone in under four hours, so we need to get going."

He got out of bed and grabbed his shirt from where it lay near her feet. "Do you have any idea what this one bit of hair does to me?" he said, tugging at a lock of hair that fell across her forehead.

"What are you talking about?"

"It sort of slides over your eye and it's so sexy I want to die."

"Come on."

"I'm serious," he said, though he was smiling. "Sometimes you sort of blow on it to get it out of the way, but that never works. Depending on whether your hands are full you ignore it or toss your head. And then sometimes you stick a barrette in it and I just want to drag you to the ground and have my way with you."

"But not die?"

"I want to have my way with you, then die. No sense in doing it the other way around."

"No. No sense at all."

His hands came up to stroke her from shoulders to wrists. "You'll stay with me the next couple of nights."

It was more a statement than a question, but she answered it anyway. She had just two nights left in Austin before she headed back to Las Vegas. She wasn't about to say no to his offer.

"I think that can be arranged."

Less than fifteen minutes later they were on the road, Jesse at the wheel. She studied the tendons in his forearm as he drove, the dark circles under his eyes from lack of sleep. For the first time she sat beside him as his lover. That gave her the right to study him, at least she thought it did, but still there were limits to what she could reveal. If only she could put some kind of limit on how much she felt.

Maybe she wouldn't have to. Maybe he'd ask her to stay for good.

It was a terrible hope, all the more so because she wasn't even sure he was good for her.

"You must be excited to be going home after all this time," she said.

He looked at her and gave a distracted smile. "I miss Austin, and I'm definitely ready for a break. I'll miss our drives, though."

"Me too."

They didn't say much the rest of the way. Most of what she was thinking couldn't be said out loud and Jesse was deep in thought. Whether he was thinking over a new song, worrying about tonight, or wondering about the two of them, there was no telling.

He kept his lucky hat next to him through the Rolling Stone interview, but he didn't need luck. The journalist admired his music and was more interested in hearing about his influences and plans for the next album than in prying into his personal life. The other interviews were conducted by journalists immersed in the local scene and were much more casual. By the time Jesse did his radio spot, he was as relaxed as if he'd been in his own living room. Beth just sat back and watched him do his thing. She could only imagine how good it felt to come home after conquering the country like he had.

The band was already at the club when they arrived for soundcheck. Will gave thpem a long look, but it wasn't the glare he might have given even a week ago, and he looked away without saying anything.

A crowd of friends and family was already milling around backstage and there was a feeling of heightened anticipation. She met Brian's wife and Stu's girlfriend, as well as Pete, the guy who'd had her job before he broke his foot. He was pretty much what she'd expected – scruffy and thin with morose eyes.

"It's nice to meet you," she said, shaking his hand. "How's your leg?"

"Fine." He heaved a sigh. "It turned out to be just a sprain, but Stu wouldn't take me back even after it was better. He said you had things under control."

"Oh. I suppose so. It didn't always feel that way, though."

"So are you and Jesse a thing?"

"What?"

"Matt said–"

"Excuse me, I need to ask Stu something," she said, forcing a smile as she hurried away.

"I see you met Pete," Jesse said, catching her by the arm. "Did a wave of depression descend while you were talking to him?"

She laughed. "Pretty much."

"And you're not even hung over." He smiled into her eyes, the same smile he'd given her that morning before he'd slipped inside her.

Her breathing stopped, maybe her heart, too. He looked like he was about to kiss her, right there in front of everyone.

"Hey, babe! Long time no see," a tall red-headed woman said, throwing her arms around him.

She wore almost the same thing Beth wore – jeans, cowboy boots, and a t-shirt, only her shirt was tighter and she oozed sex in a way Beth never could.

"Hey, Tammy. How's it going?" Jesse asked, returning the hug and kissing her on the cheek. "This is Beth. She's been on the road with us."

"Oh, hey," Tammy said, giving Beth a big smile. "I know all about you. You've been singing with them, right?"

"Just a couple of songs."

"Just nothin'," Tammy said, and Beth couldn't help smiling. "I don't care how pretty you are, Jesse doesn't let anyone mess with his music unless you rock. He didn't let me so much as sit in with him the whole time we dated."

There it was. She'd been gearing up for a parade of Jesse's ex-lovers, but she hadn't imagined meeting any of them in quite this way. She was surprised by the hot flare of jealousy, and even more surprised when it died a quick death. Tammy was nice and pretty, which only meant Jesse had good taste. And really, it was much better to know for sure he'd slept with her than to wonder.

The greenroom was crowded by this time and Beth was busy meeting the bands' friends and family. A few people from Jesse's record label and other assorted industry professionals had also turned up. It was all a little overwhelming and she wasn't sure she was up to all the schmoozing, but Jesse introduced her to everyone like she was something special, the way he might have if she were his girlfriend. She caught the curious looks people gave each other, those looks that wondered what exactly was going on between them.

What indeed.

A bunch of people went out to a nearby barbecue place for dinner and she ended up at the other end of the table from Jesse. She spent the meal talking to the musicians on either side of her and steeling glances at Jesse when she could.

The crowd was amped that night, like a hometown welcoming back its winning team. Jesse had told her they'd played Austin more times than he could count, and it showed. It felt almost like a house party, like everyone knew each other. Maybe they did.

"Ya'll are in for a treat tonight," Jesse said, in his element.

He was about to call her up, but everything seemed to be going too fast, speeding by her before she was ready for it. She felt like they'd only played one or two songs, but already it was the second set.

"You might have seen us before," Jesse said, "but you haven't seen our special guest. We've been real lucky to have her on tour with us. She's the only thing that kept me sane, matter of fact. So let's give it up for Beth Levine folks."

Jesse took her hand and smiled at her like he did every night, and when the band kicked in she felt like she'd entered a dream she'd had over and over without ever getting to the end. She gave it her best, but it all felt too unreal and she didn't quite connect with him like she usually did. Not that anyone seemed to notice. The crowd loved it and Jesse kissed her on the cheek and squeezed her hand. She left the stage to cheers and cries for more.

But there were times you could demand more till your voice gave out and it didn't mean you'd get it.

Jesse's record label threw the after party as thanks for staying with them when he could have gone to a bigger label. Instead of taking place backstage it took over the whole club and included an open bar. That, more than anything, told her how well he was doing.

She spent the first forty-five minutes of the party tallying merchandise sales and packing up. Stu got pulled away by a guy from the record label so she was busy carting boxes out to the van herself. She turned around from putting the first armload into the van and came face to face with Jesse carrying the last few boxes. He pushed them into the van and shut the door.

"What are you doing out here?" she asked. "You're the man of the hour."

"I wanted to help you. And get you alone."

He was giving her one of those looks, the kind that made all her muscles soften like she was surrendering. Preparing to be plundered. Goosebumps rose on her arms at the way his voice had gone all low and rough. His hands grabbed her hips and pulled her to him and the lust that swept through her was instantaneous.

She had time to draw one breath before he took her mouth, his hunger and impatience vibrating though him. Wrapping her arms around his back she pulled him close until there wasn't a breath of air between their bodies.

He stroked deep, demanding a response before retreating, making her come after him. She ran her hands up his arms, memorizing the way his muscles tensed at her touch. They skimmed under his shirt to find him lightly filmed with sweat and trembling.

When he finally pulled back her hands balled into fists, as if she could contain the feelings, keep them from shooting out her fingertips and bringing everything down around her ears.

His breath was ragged when he spoke. "You should stay."

Her heart kicked up, pounding in her chest at the words. She had to make sure she understood him. "What do you mean?"

"Stay in Austin. We could have more time together, and there's plenty of work now that things are breaking open for me. Stu's already looking to hire people. I'm sure there'd be something cool you could do. Maybe you could even be my business manager."

She pulled back, a hollow ache opening in her stomach.

"I can't do that."

"Why not? It'd be fun." He smiled, the way he had when he was trying to get her to sing on stage. "You don't have a another job waiting for you, and Stu would hire you in a second. It'd be perfect."

Beth stared at him, the first rush of pleasure that he wanted to see more of her stamped out by what he was actually saying. And what he wasn't. "Are you asking me to be with you, or offering me a job?"

His panicked look said it all.

God, she was so stupid. He didn't have feelings for her, certainly nothing that compared with what she felt for him.

She concentrated on breathing, willing herself not to fall apart. "Is that what you think I'd want? To *work* for you? Everything has revolved around you the last four weeks, but that's not real life, Jesse. At least, not how I want my life to be. I'm twenty-eight years old. I have a career."

"Fine, I get it. I'm sorry I said anything."

His eyes were wary and he looked stiff and uncomfortable, as if she were a reporter who'd asked too many personal questions. They stood there without saying anything, the intimacy of the past days burned away.

"I guess I'd better get back inside," he finally said. "You coming?"

"In a minute."

He hesitated, like he was going to say something else, then shook his head and went inside, closing the door carefully behind him. It was a warm night but she was suddenly freezing. She waited outside until there was no chance of running into him and then headed straight to the bathroom where she finger combed her hair and slicked on lipstick, trying to make herself look presentable. Her reflection showed swollen lips and flushed skin, but her eyes told a different story. Would anyone notice, or could she fake her way through for another hour or so?

After a few deep breaths she headed for the party, only to stop in the doorway, unable to go any farther. Throngs of people drank and ate and laughed while a cluster of musicians played on stage. It was loud and vibrant, a celebration she didn't have the heart to join.

Her eyes searched the crowded room for Jesse, finally spotting him in a cluster of musicians near the stage, a guitar slung around his neck. He was about to play, so he'd be occupied and wouldn't notice she wasn't there for a while yet.

She drank him in one last time, letting herself admire his loose-limbed grace, the way his dark hair fell into his eyes, his broad shoulders and long lean muscles. Maybe it was cowardly to leave, but then so be it. She'd reached the end of the road with Jesse.

***

Jesse looked around the hall for the millionth time, but still so sign of Beth. "I'll be back in a minute," he said, extricating himself from the clump of people hanging on his every word.

He was too distracted to be any fun and he hated that they seemed amazed no matter what lame thing he said. He found Stu talking to a producer who'd agreed to work on the next album.

"Have you seen Beth?"

Stu shook his head, distracted. "Not for a while. Listen, Paul's got some great ideas for the sessions. I think–"

"Later, okay?"

He did another scan of the room, then left the hall and walked back toward where he'd last seen her. Finally, desperate, he opened the door to the women's bathroom a crack and called her name.

A tall blond he'd talked to earlier in the night came to the door.

"No one in here but me, baby, but you can call me Beth if you like."

"I don't think so."

He turned away, pacing the hall while he tried to think where to look. He practically ran to the back door, his heart pumping hard and fast as he flung it open.

Her car was gone.

He kicked the door so that it slammed against the wall and ricocheted back at him, then kicked it again. He stood there feeling light-headed, his chest heaving as he tried to make sense of the night.

She couldn't really be gone. Maybe she just needed to get away for a bit. Probably she'd be back soon and they'd sort everything out. The thought calmed him down enough that he headed back toward the party, stopping first to get his electric guitar.

A folded piece of paper fluttered to the floor when he opened the case. At first he thought it was an old set list, but it wasn't the right paper for that. His hands shook as he opened it, and he read it over and over before he finally understood she wasn't coming back.

Keep writing your songs, Jesse. I'll be listening for them.

Chapter Twelve

"Yoo hoo. Earth to Beth."

Beth looked over at Cheryl. "Sorry. What did you say?"

They were examining wedding dresses in a budget bridal shop. Already they'd pulled eleven possible dresses between them. Cheryl was tiny, so they were looking for something relatively simple that wouldn't overwhelm her.

"I asked how you were doing."

"I'm okay I guess. I just need to stop thinking I'm going to hear from him. It's over and done with, and I'm the one that left, so I need to get over it."

She still felt guilty over how she'd run away, but it had been pure self-preservation. It wasn't just that she loved him and knew he didn't love her back. He cared enough that it would have been tempting to stay just to take what she could get. And that's what scared her. She couldn't give up everything for a man. Not again, not even if he loved her. She'd never forgive herself, or him, if she did.

He'd called her several times while she was still in town but she'd let them all go to voicemail. He'd sounded by turns sorry, angry and confused. He'd wanted to see her again, but she'd taken the coward's way out and left town without speaking to him.

She hadn't heard from him since, and no wonder.

She thought about him constantly, though. About the times they sang together in the car, like they were the only two people in the world. How he looked at her when they were on stage, how he said her name when he was inside her.

She hadn't seen him for five weeks and it hadn't gotten any easier.

She stood up and resumed looking through the racks. "Stu emailed me the other day. They're releasing a live version of one of the songs we sang together."

"Oh my God. That's incredible."

"It is pretty cool. I'll even make money from it." She paused. "Also, I've been getting occasional queries from people who want to represent me."

"Are you serious? Like, representing you in your musical career?"

"It doesn't matter. I'm not interested in any of that."

"Really? Not even a little?"

"Nope. I liked singing with Jesse, but that's as far as it goes. He made it easy, but I'm not interested in trying to make a career of it." She sighed and sat down. There were many conveniently placed chairs located around the store. Maybe people wedding dress shopping were prone to weariness. "I miss it, though. Life seems so empty now. Every day was an adventure with him, and I felt...it sounds so lame, but I felt more alive with him."

"That's not lame. That's love."

"I guess so, but I never felt that with anyone else. What am I supposed to do? What if I never meet anyone who makes me feel like he did?"

Cheryl seemed to think that over. "You won't find another Jesse, but you'll find a guy who's great in other ways, one who's able to give you everything you deserve. Someone who doesn't let you down. But it's too soon to think about that. I think you need to focus on other things that make you happy."

"Like my new idea."

She'd been researching how to become a business manager for artists since her return to Las Vegas.

"Exactly. You just need to lose yourself in something you're passionate about."

"I think I'd be perfect for it. I had a couple of artist clients at my old firm, a painter and a dancer. They were in a totally different boat from people who work more regular jobs. Plus I'd handle contracts when they're setting up tours and signing record deals. I have a lot to learn, but I could get where I need to be, and it helps that I know the business from the other side. I think that'll be a real asset."

"I'd hire you."

Beth stopped and looked at her friend, her hands falling to her sides. She'd gotten kind of carried away, but at least she'd been thinking of something other than Jesse. It felt good to get excited about something she had control over.

"Enough about me. Let's find you a dress."

***

Jesse listened to the playback and wished like hell there wasn't a roomful of people waiting on his reaction.

They'd been recording for three weeks and they had five songs in the bag already. Brian and Matt were back, and they had awesome session musicians sitting in on guitar, horns and fiddle. The problems had come when they started recording "Better Off."

Mary Ann was a great singer. He'd heard her before and admired her work, but something was off. They'd been trying everything and he was starting to feel like an ass. He tried to explain what he wanted from her, but it was a quality he was looking for, a style, and how could you tell someone to alter the essence of how they sang? He'd asked her to try her part a few different ways and she'd done exactly what he asked, but it still wasn't what he wanted, and he couldn't pretend it was.

Just like he couldn't pretend that Lisa or Michelle had sounded the way he wanted.

His displeasure must have been obvious, because her shoulders slumped and she started biting her lip and looking like she might cry. Behind him Matt gave a low groan. It was after ten and they'd been going at it since noon. Everyone was exhausted. He'd kept them there too long trying for something he couldn't explain. It was costing money and cutting into the budget for the rest of the songs, which meant he was putting the album in jeopardy.

Stu stood near the sound engineer on the other side of the glass, frowning, his arms crossed over his chest while they listened to the playback. When it was done he beckoned Jesse out of the studio.

Jesse followed him down the hall and out into the parking lot.

Stu planted his feet and crossed his arms like he meant business. "What's going on? Everyone else thought that take was dead on."

"Well, I guess you're not hearing what I'm hearing."

"She's the third singer we've had in here, Jesse. We can't afford any more delays. These women are all excellent and they've done exactly what you asked."

"I'm just not getting the sound I want. It doesn't feel right."

"What *would* feel right? Beth?"

Jesse walked a few feet away, not sure how to answer. What the hell was he doing, really? Had he been trying fruitlessly to make these women sound like Beth?

Fucking hell.

"She's what I hear in my head," he admitted. "Nothing else sounds right."

"Okay, now we're getting somewhere," Stu said, nodding like he was encouraged by his revelation. "The question is, can you adjust your expectations, or do we get Beth in here?"

The thought of seeing her, of having a reason to call and ask her to come, sent his heart racing. In the five weeks since he last saw her he hadn't gone a whole hour without thinking about her. But he was also scared of seeing her and wanting her too much, of seeing in her eyes she didn't feel the same. Scared of wanting her without having any way to keep her.

He'd hurt her, that was obvious. Well, it hadn't been obvious immediately, because he was an idiot, but she must have cared about him or she wouldn't have been so upset at his lame-ass offer. She wouldn't have run away and ignored his calls.

He needed to try harder. Needed to see her, touch her, sing with her again.

He waited until he was back home, then he sat down and stared at his phone. Would she even pick up, or was she so mad she'd ignore his call? What would he say if it went to voicemail?

Christ, he'd never been one to over-think things, but he was making himself crazy. He dialed her number.

"Hello?"

That husky voice. He'd been hearing that voice in his dreams, whispering in his ear.

"Beth. It's Jesse."

"I know." He could hear her wariness. "Is something wrong?"

"Kind of, but not like in a life or death way." He stopped and huffed out a nervous laugh. "Actually, it feels like life or death to me."

"What's going on?"

He took a deep breath and prayed he could make his plea sound appealing rather than desperate. "Well, the thing is, I'm recording, and we've kind of hit a snag. I'm hoping you can help out."

"How would I do that?"

"It's about 'Better Off.' We're trying to finish the track. I've tried three different singers, but it's...they're not you."

"Oh."

He rushed on. "Stu's about ready to kill me. Hell, everyone's about ready to kill me, and I can't blame them. But I just want to record the best version, the one I hear in my head, and that means you."

"I don't think that's a good idea."

"Just think about it. We'd put you up in a nice hotel, you'd get paid for your time and a cut of the royalties."

"I'm sorry, I can't."

That was it. No explanation, nothing about another job she couldn't get away from. Which meant she didn't want to.

He searched for a way to keep her talking. "Did Stu tell you about the live recording? We're releasing it on YouTube, just like you suggested."

"I didn't realize there'd be a video. What show is it from?"

"The Flagstaff show. There were other good nights, but that was the best."

She was quiet on the other end, but at least she hadn't hung up yet.

He tried again. "You were really something, you know that? It's not like I didn't know it, but looking back at the footage…"

"I didn't realize anyone was filming us," she said.

"Neither did I, but one of Stu's friends did it on a whim and showed it to him later. It's not perfect since he wasn't up there with us, but you get the feel of it."

"I should probably go, but it was good to hear from you. I'm sorry I can't help."

"No, I get it. You didn't sign up for that. I had to ask, though."

"Take care, Jesse."

"Right. You too, Beth."

He kept the phone pressed to his ear in case by some miracle she didn't hang up. But she did. He whipped the phone across the room and was almost disappointed when it bounced off the wall and landed without breaking.

He was an idiot. What woman would get on a plane to do a favor for a guy who'd treated her like some dumb groupie? He must have been delusional to think Beth would go for that. She'd made it clear she wasn't going to let her life revolve around him anymore.

Which left him with one last option. He'd go to her.

***

"Look, I was all for bringing her here, but going out there is insane. We're paying out the nose for studio time here, for Christ's sake."

It was three in the morning and he and Stu were eating at an all-night diner around the corner from the studio. Jesse had expected an argument from Stu, so he took this in stride.

"I just need a couple of days. You can lay down some of the extra drums and guitar while I'm gone."

Stu stared at him. "You're telling me you'll leave your own session. If I had suggested that you'd have taken my head off."

"Well, yeah, normally I would want to be there. But this is an emergency. Anyway, we can always do them over if I don't like it."

Stu grunted. "So I'm supposed to find you a studio in Vegas for when?"

"Next weekend."

"Wonderful. That should be easy." He sighed and wiped his mouth. Half his omelet was still on his plate, but he looked too tired to finish it.

Jesse ignored his sarcasm. "It's just a couple of tracks. I can handle that."

Stu signaled the waitress for another coffee. "I'll make some calls tomorrow."

"Thanks, man. I owe you."

"You've been owing me for years."

Jesse didn't argue.

Stu took a deep swallow of his refreshed coffee. "She called me a couple of weeks ago."

"What? Who called you?"

"Beth, Jesse. Who do you think we're talking about?"

"Why would she call you?"

"She's setting up her business and wanted to know if I'd be a reference. I said I would and told her I'd keep my ears open for her."

"Why didn't you tell her we'd hire her?"

Stu closed his eyes, as if Jesse were wearing him out.

"It's not such a stupid idea," Jesse said, pressing his advantage. If that's what it was when Stu looked like he was giving up. "She knows the business now, she knows us. She's got the right background and she's smart. We could do a lot worse."

"It just so happens I agree. But she's not interested in working for us. She said so."

He didn't have an answer for that. It was starting to look like Beth didn't want anything to do with him, a thought that started an ache in his chest he couldn't ignore.

The next Friday afternoon Jesse sat in a rented car, listening to music while waiting for Beth to come home. He'd been sitting there for two hours already, the coffee he'd drunk souring in his nervous stomach.

It didn't help that he felt like a stalker, and that she was almost certain to be pissed. What he was doing was manipulative as well as desperate. It was just beginning to hit him that neither of those things would make him more appealing.

He shifted in his seat and was just starting to contemplate a run to the bathroom at the Starbucks down the block when a familiar Subaru pulled into the parking lot. The door opened and one red booted foot came out, then the other. Then the rest of her appeared, as beautiful as ever.

His heart slammed against his ribs and his breath came fast and light. For a few seconds he wondered if he might actually pass out.

Beth leaned into the back seat and came back out with a couple of reusable bags full of groceries. There was a lot of food there. What if she was cooking for someone else? A man?

He watched her cross the parking lot and enter a stairway, then reappear on the catwalk two stories up. She rested one bag on her bent thigh as she unlocked the door and disappeared inside.

He waited a few minutes, then got out of the car and retraced her steps until he was at her door, feeling the whole time like he was about to go onstage in front of an audience that had paid to see someone else. He wiped his palms on his jeans and knocked.

The blue curtain in front of the little window on the door parted and Beth peered out at him. He couldn't have actually heard her gasp, but her eyes widened, and then thank God she was opening the door.

Chapter Thirteen

Jesse. At her door. Looking so good she could have wept. Or laughed hysterically. She wanted to throw him on her bed and ravage him, and she wanted to hit him.

"Hey, Beth."

God, that voice. That alone was almost enough to make her forget everything and let him in, no questions asked. But that meant she was still susceptible to him, and that wasn't good.

Her head felt light, as if she'd stood up too quickly, so she held onto the door and tried to think what to do. He looked nervous, like he thought she might shut the door in his face, but this was Jesse. He'd been kind of a jerk at the end, but mostly he'd hurt her without realizing it.

She stepped back. "Come in."

He was wearing a brown leather jacket that fell to his hips and hung open on the blue western-style shirt with snaps she'd always loved. And of course worn jeans and his beat-up cowboy boots. His hair was a little longer than it had been when she last saw him, but he was clean-shaven. Had he done that for her?

He smiled one of his crooked smiles and walked across the threshold. His eyes never left her, and she was reminded again of how focused on her he always was. No one else did that, and she felt herself flush as her heart picked up its pace.

The heat between them was still there, that connection she'd convinced herself was all in her head. She stepped back another few inches and crossed her arms over her chest.

"What are you doing here?"

"I figured I'd have a better chance of seeing you if I didn't give you a chance to tell me not to come."

Then he flashed her one of his full-bore smiles, unleashing all the charm and charisma and sex he used on stage in front of hundreds of people. Only now it landed on her alone in an apartment too tiny to contain it.

"You look good, honey."

Ah, there it was. She had to resist the urge to close her eyes at the sweet sound of it.

They were still standing in the little hallway inside Cheryl's apartment, just a few feet from the living room. She wasn't planning on inviting him in, but he moved by her and somehow she couldn't stop him. He didn't sit down, though. Instead he prowled around, looking at pictures and knickknacks. Restless, that same energy he'd always had coming off him.

He was frowning, like he was trying to make sense of the framed diploma on the wall and the pictures of Cheryl and Jason.

"This is Cheryl's apartment," she explained. "She moved in with Jason, but I'm staying here and finishing out the lease. We haven't gotten around to moving all her stuff out since I don't have my own things yet."

That seemed to satisfy him, for the moment at least.

"What is it you want, Jesse?"

"I rented some studio space here so you could record."

"What are you talking about?"

He shoved his hands into his coat pockets and looked at her with all the determination and stubbornness she recognized from times on the tour when he'd fought for his own way.

"I want you on this album, Beth. It just isn't right without you. So I figured I'd make it easy. You'll make some decent money, too."

"Jesse—"

"It should only take a few hours, and we booked the studio for two days so we can do it whenever you're free."

He was making it impossible to refuse, which was obviously what he'd planned. Maybe she was putting up too much of a fight. He'd come all this way for her to sing, why shouldn't she just do it? It's not like he'd treated her badly or done something terrible. Anyway, she'd always hated the idea of another woman singing those songs.

She let out her breath. "Okay, I'll do it."

"You will?" he asked, surprise and delight beaming from him.

"Yes, I will." God help her. "I'm free tomorrow after one."

"That's perfect. I'll come pick you up."

"You don't have to do that. Tell me where it is and I'll meet you there."

"I'll pick you up," he repeated.

"Fine. I'll see you then."

He hesitated, like he wanted to say more. She needed him to leave so she could be alone to scream or cry, so she stood there with her arms crossed and didn't give him anything more.

He gave her one of his wry smiles, his mouth turning up on one side, only this time he just looked sad. It was all she could do not to call him back, but she kept silent and watched him leave.

***

By twelve-fifty the next day she was pacing the apartment from couch to window to bathroom mirror. She'd been in a state since he left the day before and she was no better now. As much as she tried to deny her feelings for him, they were as strong as the day she left Austin.

It had taken her an hour to dress, only to end up in jeans and a turtleneck sweater, and she'd put on and taken off her red cowboy boots three or four times before finally leaving them on. They gave her confidence and made her feel good, and that's what she needed today. Hopefully Jesse didn't take them as some sort of signal.

She spent a few more minutes warming up, then his car pulled into the parking lot and she went out and closed the door behind her. Jesse smiled up at her through the bars of the walkway, and just like that her heart betrayed her, stupidly swelling with joy at the sight of him.

He opened her door for her and waited while she got in, then climbed in the other side. He hadn't missed the boots, but he didn't say anything. Was it because she was freezing him out? She couldn't help that, though. It was self-protection, and she needed it.

"Have you been singing at all since you got back?" he finally asked.

"Just around the house."

He said nothing more and she was left with the feeling that he was hoping for something else from her. The silence that enveloped them was deep and wide, nothing like the comfortable quiet they used to share.

"How are the guys?" she asked, unable to bear it.

"Fine. I found someone else to play bass after Will bowed out, but Matt and Brian are recording."

She nodded her head, unable to think of more to say.

"Stu tells me you're starting your own business, just like you planned."

"It's a lot of work to get going, but I'm excited about it."

"You'll be great."

A short time later they entered a residential neighborhood, nearly every house covered in Christmas lights and wreaths. She still hadn't gotten used to seeing all that in the middle of the desert. Everything seemed so forced, so bleak, but maybe that was just her.

"This is where the studio is?" she asked.

"Stu knows someone who knows someone who has a studio in his house. It's mostly for private use but he's doing us a favor. It won't be anything like I usually record in, but it'll be just fine for what we need."

He pulled up in front of a white two-story and they were greeted at the door by a bearded man in his fifties who reeked of pot and led them downstairs into a basement studio. Beth stood by while Henry and Jesse talked, only half understanding what they said. Not that it mattered. Her job was to sing when they told her to.

A little while later she stood next to Jesse in front of a microphone, her anxiety escalating. What if she couldn't get back into the rhythm of things? What if after all this trouble she sounded terrible?

Henry sat down at his soundboard and tested their mic levels, then handed them each a set of headphones.

"We already recorded 'Better Off' and 'Down by the River'" Jesse explained. "All we need now are your parts, but I figured I'd sing, too. If I sound better today than what I already recorded we can use it."

"Hey, Henry," Jesse called across the room, "can you play 'Better Off'" once through for her?"

Henry nodded and Beth adjusted her headphones. Moments later the song came on and she was right back there, her whole world Jesse and the tour and her spiraling feelings. She closed her eyes and tried not to think about the moment she knew she was in love with him.

When she opened her eyes Jesse was watching her.

"All set?"

She nodded, afraid to speak.

The song played again, this time without Jesse's part, but it sounded distant and strange, like it was being piped in from some other planet. He looked right at her as he sang and she answered like she always had, meeting him in that nowhere space between them. Only this time it was so terrifying she tried to lock down all the feelings it threatened to pull from her.

She sounded terrible.

Jesse signaled Henry to stop and took off his headphones.

"Everything all right?" he asked.

She nodded and tried to smile. "It just feels strange."

"We'll take it easy and work our way into it, okay?"

Oh God, what had she gotten herself into? For weeks she'd been remembering how it felt to sing with Jesse, and now she was with him again and all the dangers of it came back to her. She should never have agreed to this.

She made herself breathe. This wasn't going to work unless she gave it all she had. He was looking for what she'd done before and she could either do it or run away.

But she couldn't run away, because as awful as it was, she wanted this.

Henry cued the song up and it began to play again. Jesse's smile for her was one of whole-hearted belief, and then he started to sing, his mournful voice coming to her through the headset with no way to distance herself from it.

She watched him, letting him lead her into the song because he was the anchor and the only way through it, he was the troubadour and the pied piper, the heartbreaker.

The song cracked her open, leaving her vulnerable to every note, every feeling. She came in on cue and held nothing back, and all the while she remembered the delicious scrape of his unshaven jaw on her throat, the even fiercer friction of his calloused fingertips tracing along her skin, his voice calling her name, urgent and hungry. Everything that was in his song made real, and she sang it with him now, reliving it all. Her voice wove around his, sweetening the dark notes, trembling over the sorrowful ones.

She'd never felt more exposed, more vulnerable. And yet there was nothing for it. There was no holding back with him, no going halfway with Jesse, now or ever. That was the curse and the thrill of being with him.

He never took his eyes off her as they sang what felt like an elegy for their own short affair. The whole arc of their unlived relationship unfolding in a song he'd written before he'd met her. But once again it became her heartbreak, her regret.

She barely made it through. Tears were rolling down her cheeks as she sang the last verse, and as soon as Henry signaled she pulled her headset off and ran for the stairs. She threw open the front door and ran outside, only to stop and look wildly around. She had no idea where she was, but it was miles from home. Maybe she could walk until she found a busier street and then hitchhike…

Jesse burst through the door and ran down the steps, stopping in front of her to take her by the shoulders. "Beth, honey, what is it?"

She pushed him away, hating that she was crying, that he'd see what he did to her. "I'm not doing this. Take me home."

"What's wrong? I don't under–"

"You shouldn't have come here. I don't care about your stupid songs. I don't want to see you anymore."

He went pale, his lips pressing into a thin line. "Don't say that. Give me a chance to explain."

"There's nothing to say."

"I didn't come here for the songs, not the way you think."

It was painful to look at him and impossible to look away. Just his hands on her filled her with a crushing hope.

"I brought you here because I wanted you to remember what it was like between us. How good we were together."

"It was easy, then. Everything I did was for you."

"No, that's not why. You know it's not. We have something."

"Don't you think I know that, Jesse? But it wasn't enough for you."

"I was an idiot, but I was trying to keep you the only way I knew how, and it didn't seem like you wanted me."

"I felt like such a fool," she said, all the hurt of their last night together coming back to her.

His face fell. "I'm sorry I hurt you, honey. I can't tell you how sorry I am."

He took her hand and held it between both of his, instantly warming her. The contact felt good and right, but still tenuous, still easily broken.

He let out a shaky breath. "I offered you a job because I wanted you to be part of my life, not because I think the world revolves around me." He grimaced and shook his head. "Hell, maybe I do, but that wasn't what I meant by it. I wanted you to stay, and I thought if you were still working with me you wouldn't resent what I do."

"But you know I didn't."

"Every single girlfriend I've ever had resented it. It takes me away for months at a time, for one thing. And you know how there are girls everywhere. No one ever trusted me."

"Should they have?" she asked, looking him straight in the eye, terrified of what she'd see there.

His gaze was unwavering. "I've never cheated on anyone, but I never gave my heart to anyone, either. All I needed was my music. But it's not enough anymore. None of it's enough unless I have you."

"What are you saying?"

"I'm saying I love you."

She stared at him, trying to take it in, afraid to believe what she was hearing.

"I know I look like a bad bet," he rushed on. "But it could work, I know it could. We're good together, and Austin would be a great place for your business. You'd love it there, and you could come on tour whenever you wanted. I'll write more songs for you. For us."

He took her face in his hands, the rough pads of his thumbs wiping away the tears. "You won't have to compromise to be with me, Beth. I'll make sure all the doors fly open for you."

She had no defense against him anymore, and she didn't need it. Instead of trying not to feel anything, she took a deep breath and let herself feel everything.

"I would love that," she said, smiling all her love up at him.

He looked stunned. "You would?"

"I love you, Jesse. Of course I want all those things. I just didn't want to be like all the other women who throw themselves at you."

"It was never like that for us."

"I hoped it wasn't."

He rested his forehead against hers and wrapped his arms around her. She held him close and breathed him in, her head still trying to catch up to her heart. His lips touched her jaw, her cheek, her eyelids. Finally he kissed her properly.

She was out of breath the next time she spoke. "Hey, Jesse?"

"Yeah, honey?"

"What do you say we go finish those songs.

One Year Later

Melbourne, Australia

Beth stood offstage, smiling at the sight of Jesse in his lucky cowboy hat singing to the packed crowd. Even jet-lagged the band sounded great, and Jesse was so excited by his first non-US performance, he'd barely been able to sit still all day. A few hours in bed that afternoon had been a useful distraction. She'd had her way with him and left him sleeping soundly to answer emails from the manager of a band she was working with.

That was the great thing about her job. She could do most of it from wherever she wanted, so traveling now and then wasn't a big deal. She'd even found a couple of new clients on the road.

"This one's brand new," Jesse said, his voice reverberating around the huge concert hall. He strummed his guitar, picking out the first few bars. "In fact, I haven't sung it live yet, so I hope you'll be gentle."

He grinned and waited for the wild applause to die down. "I'm gonna need some help with this one, so I want ya'll to give it up for my wife, Beth."

He turned toward her, the look in his eye just for her. "Come on out here, honey. You know I can't do it without you."

ABOUT THE AUTHOR

Isabel began reading romances at the age of fourteen. That's the year her grandmother came to visit, bringing with her a shopping bag filled with (very tame) Harlequin and Silhouette romance novels. Isabel was immediately and forever hooked. What could be better than experiencing all that lust and new love just by reading a book?

Sign up for Isabel's newsletter at www.isabelmorin.com[1] and get new release alerts and exclusive content. Your email address will never be shared, and you can unsubscribe at any time.

Email Isabel at isabel@isabelmorin.com. She'd love to hear from you!

---

1. http://www.isabelmorin.com

www.ingramcontent.com/pod-product-compliance
Lightning Source LLC
Chambersburg PA
CBHW061442150726
47987CB00001B/310